Flying Saucers

Images of Elsewhere

Vol. I

PETER LANG
Oxford - Berlin - Bruxelles - Chennai - Lausanne - New York

Flying Saucers

An Introduction

Timothy Jenkins

PETER LANG
Oxford · Berlin · Bruxelles · Chennai · Lausanne · New York

Bibliographic information published by the Deutsche Nationalbibliothek.
The German National Library lists this publication in the German National Bibliography;
detailed bibliographic data is available on the Internet at http://dnb.d-nb.de.

A catalogue record for this book is available from the British Library.

Library of Congress Cataloging-in-Publication Data

Names: Jenkins, Timothy, 1952- author.
Title: Flying saucers : an introduction / Timothy Jenkins.
Other titles: Images of elsewhere
Description: Oxford ; New York : Peter Lang, [2025]- | Includes the text
  from a U.S. Air Force report on unidentified flying objects. | Includes
  bibliographical references and index. | Contents: vol. 1 Images of
  elsewhere
Identifiers: LCCN 2024031351 (print) | LCCN 2024031352 (ebook) | ISBN
  9781803741581 (paperback ; v. 1) | ISBN 9781803741598 (ebook ; v. 1) |
  ISBN 9781803741604 (epub ; v. 1)
Subjects: LCSH: Unidentified flying objects—Sightings and
  encounters—Social aspects. | Unidentified flying
  objects—Research—United States. | Social psychology. |
  Geopolitics—Psychological aspects. | United States. Air
  Force—History—20th century. | United States. Air Force—Technological
  innovations.
Classification: LCC TL789 .J463 2025 (print) | LCC TL789 (ebook) | DDC
  001.942—dc23/eng/20240723
LC record available at https://lccn.loc.gov/2024031351
LC ebook record available at https://lccn.loc.gov/2024031352

Cover image: Line drawing by the author.
Cover design by Peter Lang Group AG

ISBN 978-1-80374-158-1 (print)
ISBN 978-1-80374-159-8 (ePDF)
ISBN 978-1-80374-160-4 (ePub)
DOI 10.3726/b20795

© 2025 Peter Lang Group AG, Lausanne
Published by Peter Lang Ltd, Oxford, United Kingdom
info@peterlang.com - www.peterlang.com

Timothy Jenkins has asserted his right under the Copyright, Designs and Patents Act, 1988,
to be identified as Author of this Work.

All rights reserved.
All parts of this publication are protected by copyright.
Any utilisation outside the strict limits of the copyright law, without the permission of the
publisher, is forbidden and liable to prosecution.
This applies in particular to reproductions, translations, microfilming, and storage and processing
in electronic retrieval systems.

This publication has been peer reviewed.

Contents

Series Preface	vii
Acknowledgements	xi
Introduction	1

CHAPTER 1
Making sense of flying saucer reports — 5

CHAPTER 2
Technology and the categories of experience — 35

CHAPTER 3
The Report on Unidentified Flying Objects — 65

Bibliography	155
Index	159

Series Preface

Reports of flying saucers – also known as UFOs – constitute a puzzle, for they are numerous, well attested, and hard to believe. There are tempting shortcuts to a 'solution' – that the sightings are real, or mistaken, or fictitious (made up) – but none of these prove satisfactory. Instead, we are brought to consider the history of sightings and the history, also, of how it became possible to regard such incidents in the terms that have become customary. Flying saucers in this fashion become a feature of the wider society, and allow an angle of approach to our modern, technological civilization: a small-scale problem that allows insight into the larger setting.

The six essays stand as independent studies. Each deals with an aspect of the life of flying saucers or UFOs: their appearance after the Second World War within the constellation of military and technological interests, their debt to early science fiction and its sources, the development of the search for signs of extra-terrestrial intelligence, the first adoptions of the 'interplanetary hypothesis' in civilian circles, the further expansion of reports, first, of sightings and, then, of abductions in the wider society, and, finally, a review of the range of forms which have appeared. Taken together, they form a thorough enquiry into reports of sightings of flying saucers.

The series as a whole makes three contributions to resolving the puzzle posed by such reports.

First, it relates three bodies of materials from the United States in the mid-twentieth century whose interactions must be taken into consideration when speaking about flying saucers. These are the science fiction milieu, the interplay of military and technical interests, and reports of sightings by members of the public; in short, stories, military work, and ordinary lives. The first contribution is to study their interactions, overlaps, borrowings and synergies.

The second is to derive the categories that are necessary to explain the convergence of these materials. Repeating patterns appear in science fiction literature, the history of Air Force intelligence in the Cold War period, the early days of NASA, the search for extra-terrestrial intelligence, and a wide variety of incidents and claims made by members of the public. To make sense of their common nature and to see how their interactions work, we also need to investigate some intellectual history. There is a longstanding tradition of popular thought putting new scientific discoveries and technological innovation to work for human moral purposes. This tradition was taken up by military and technical interests in the middle third of the twentieth century, using three clusters of ideas: the intimate connection between military technology and the world picture offered by modern media, the concept of 'communication' (and, post-War, of 'information') that became central in the period, and an understanding of 'memory' as an exact record of the past. These ideas were shared with a wider public: in the context of international tensions, hopes of communication and fears of its breakdown were given expression in the appearance of new forms of life, forms given content by the earlier longstanding history. This is the second contribution the essay makes to the topic: an investigation of the common patterns of thought necessary for stories, military work and ordinary lives to interact.

And, last, a mechanism is proposed by which these interactions occur. This is an analysis of the ways in which these 'images', which contain both real and imaginary elements, make their appearance compelling. I find well documented instances – in particular, the sessions in which memories of abductions are recovered – where the social mechanism is uncovered that allows the oscillation between the two elements, a mechanism that can be glimpsed at work in other sites but which cannot be tracked in such detail in the documents and other sources we have concerning advances in research, security decisions, the records of incidents and so forth. This is the third contribution.

I first came to the puzzle of flying saucer reports when working on spirit messages and similar forms of social life (such as parapsychology and psychical research) and realized that the search for extra-terrestrial intelligence was the latest expression of a long-held desire for communication with disembodied minds compatible with our own. It has taken a good deal of time and work to give substance to this insight. As will be clear from my references, there is an abundance of work of the highest quality in this broad area, on which I draw to give shape to the argument. If I have contributed anything, it is by making a systematic enquiry and by putting together materials that are not always associated, and by continuing to ask questions rather than settling for accepted answers. In this fashion, I hope to have supported readers who find these topics interesting rather than those who wish to close them down, and I also hope to have contributed in some small degree to understanding the contemporary world.

Acknowledgements

Much of the preliminary work for writing up this project was undertaken during nine months at the Center of Theological Inquiry in Princeton, where I was a participant in the programme 'The Societal Implications of Astrobiology', 2016–2017. I am deeply grateful to Dr William Storrar and Dr Joshua Maudlin, the Director and Associate Director, for their hospitality and guidance, to the other participants in the programme, for their friendship and the shared intellectual environment they created, and to NASA and the John Templeton Foundation, who funded the programme.

Several paragraphs of this essay are drawn from a piece which appeared as 'The Role of Unproved Ideas in the Production of Knowledge: A Case Study', in *Re-Creating Anthropology: Sociality, Matter, and the Imagination*, edited by David N. Gellner and Dolores P. Martinez, Routledge, 2022: 126–137; they are utilized with the publisher's permission, which is gratefully acknowledged.

Introduction

The first impression, when approaching the subject of flying saucers, is one of confusion and too many leads to follow up. Confusion, given the rival claims of advocates, sceptics, and mythologists. And so many paths to explore, not only reports of sightings, Close Encounters, and abductions, but also elaborations along diverse lines including ancient or lost civilizations, paranormal mental powers such as remote sensing, potential new technologies, anti-gravity devices and the like, and the suggestion of government secret operations and cover-ups. Where can one start?

Let me make two claims, both evident enough, to identify a starting point. The first is to say that technology is crucial, and that this essay concerns an investigation into the role of technology in generating images of what we call spaceships, flying saucers, or UFOs. The second is to say we should pay attention to words, and that this essay describes the emergence of the single term 'UFO' or 'Unidentified Flying Object' in the mid-1950s. These may serve as pointers, to help orientate the reader.

In the first chapter, I clarify the object of study and then outline how to set about investigating both the object and its emergence. The object of investigation appears in taking seriously the disruptive effect of early flying saucer sightings – their combination of real and imaginative elements – and in not trying to resolve this effect by resorting to a standard set of judgements – choosing between their being real, or the result of error, or the product of fiction. We – the reader and author together – are not in the business of sorting between claims and awarding the palm to one or another of the positions. Instead, the sightings may be characterized as the combination of a new kind of object and a new way of seeing, and both components can be traced in each report; hence the 'scandal' each sighting brings with it. This combination I term an 'image'.

Then, in the second chapter, I explore the kind of world in which sightings of flying saucers emerged for the first time. This is a world of novelty: original kinds of experience and interpretation created by the interplay between new military technologies such as jet flight, rockets, radar, new fuels, new techniques of generating and analysing data, on the one hand, and new means of communication, in particular, film and radio, on the other. The characteristics of this recently created worldview – or way of living in the world – are outlined, considering the close relation between developments in weapons and in the media, the fragmentation of everyday experience and continuous time that accompanies these developments, and the popular distrust of official narratives, statements and motives that can arise in these conditions of breakdown and discontinuity.

We can then trace the emergence of the idea of the UFO – an Unidentified Flying Object – in such a world condition. This is the business of the third chapter. I use the sole book from the period that comes from within the context of Air Force intelligence work, written by the person in charge of the operation which had the task of investigating flying saucers. Reading this text, supplemented by contemporary documents that have since become available, we can follow the construction of the object in question (and its naming) in the tense political and security environment prevailing at the end of the War, marked by the development of the Cold War and the beginning of the Korean conflict, with new defence and communications technologies being invented and deployed, and as local and national conditions evolved rapidly and unpredictably. In brief, we have a case study of a text which not only contributes to the historical record but also allows us to decipher in some detail the processes going on at the time. There were two equally pressing concerns for the intelligence operation: first, to find out what flying saucers were and what to make of them; second, to control any public reaction to the idea of them and their possible presence. The story of the UFO is a response to these two concerns, a technical reply to the introduction of flying saucers into a post-War world driven by the demands of security.

By starting with such a specific, early instance, observing the reports it draws on and the synthesis it offers, and taking into account the wider context in which it emerged and elements of which it reflects, it is possible to begin to disentangle the various materials that have been taken and used in contemporary interpretations and to distinguish those which were introduced later and projected back. In sum, we can offer an introduction to the topic of flying saucers.

CHAPTER 1

Making sense of flying saucer reports

How can we make sense of flying saucer reports, of which there are thousands? These reports make claims that are at once a matter of fact and, on the face of it, highly improbable. Both those making the report and those receiving it feel alike that the claim to have seen something is not, in this case, self-explanatory; the main characteristic of such observations is that they demand further investigation: they provoke thought. It is worth hanging on to this feature because none of the obvious 'solutions' – it is real; it is a mistake; it is imaginary – resolve the puzzle.

The purpose of this first chapter is to clear some ground: to understand better the object of our investigation and to outline the approach adopted. I have included a discussion of the method adopted as an endnote. I should make clear at the outset that my concern is with flying saucers in the United States, for that is where reports and discussion of reports first appeared, and that, although my interest covers the whole period to the present, in this essay I focus on the early years, 1947–1953, for the first forms of the phenomenon set the broad terms for the later story. Here, to start, is a typical report, though of a somewhat later date.

I. A report and its implications

An Army Reserve helicopter with a crew of four under Captain Lawrence Coyne was being flown north-east from Columbus, Ohio, on 18 October 1973. They had flown to Columbus earlier in the day for routine medical examinations and were returning home to Cleveland, where the crew were based, leaving around 10:30 in the evening. At 11:00 p.m., flying at

1,200 feet over rural farmland, a crew member noticed a southbound red light. Two minutes later, a second crew member saw a bright red light appear to the east, which kept pace with the helicopter for a minute and a half. He alerted Coyne; a moment later the light changed direction, coming towards the helicopter. Coyne took over the controls and put the helicopter into a descent; he also called the nearby airport, Mansfield, with responsibility for the air space, to ask whether they had any high-performance aircraft in the area. After an initial exchange, however, radio contact failed on both UHF and VHF frequencies. The red light closed on the helicopter at a speed Coyne estimated to be 600 knots (nearly 700 mph). Fearing a collision, he pushed the control stick down, descending according to the controls from 1700 to within 700 feet of the ground. He then saw a craft looming in front of the helicopter, broadside on; it was a 'cigar-shaped, metallic structure', with a red light at the nose and a white tail light. It had neither wings nor identifying marks. Beneath the white light, there was 'a pyramid-shaped green beam [which] swept a 90-degree arc and shone through the helicopter windshield', before covering and revealing the detail of the craft. The outline was visible from the reflected light and against the stars of the night sky. The craft hovered over the helicopter silently for ten to twelve seconds before accelerating away towards the northwest. The crew could see the white rear light. The craft executed 'a sharp 45-degree turn to the right' and then the light extinguished, and the craft could no longer be seen. At this point, Coyne saw from the altimeter that, despite his action and the position of the control stick, the helicopter was at 3,500 feet and climbing at 1,000 feet a second. He *raised* the control stick and the ascent ceased at 3,800 feet 'with a slight bump'. He returned the helicopter to its previous altitude; they made radio contact without difficulty with another airbase, and the remainder of the flight passed without further incident.

An account of the crew's experience appeared in a local newspaper and provoked the interest of investigators, one of whom spoke to the witnesses three months after the event. Others undertook more extensive research, including unearthing independent witnesses. These were, first, a woman driving three adolescents in the area at the time, who saw two coordinated lights, red and green, which became a craft, and witnessed its encounter with a low flying helicopter, stopping over it. The witnesses, who were only interviewed three years later, also saw a green light flare up and illuminate the area, and described the craft's departure, flying off northwest and disappearing behind trees. A second group of witnesses, a family living close by, some fifteen years after the event recalled sounds of a helicopter close by and a green light.

A sceptic later offered elements of a natural explanation, suggesting what had been seen was a fireball from a meteor shower, and that the change of direction by the helicopter was the result of instinctive reactions by the pilot.[1]

Many elements found in this report will be repeated in other cases. For example, there is the unexplained object, an artificial machine which shows intentional behaviour (as if piloted), which is equipped with lights and displays a remarkable technical performance including high speeds, manoeuverability, abrupt stopping and accelerating away, and hovering, all without making a sound. The craft also appears to produce effects in man-made equipment, cutting radio communication and taking over the helicopter's controls. Then, we have to evaluate the human testimonies, taken from four servicemen in the first place and backed by independent witnesses, all of whom on the surface appear reliable people capable of maintaining responsible roles in their ordinary lives. The technical tone of the summary might be added to the list: the precise date, the details of time, estimations of speed and distance, the impersonal voice. Last, there is the reception of these reports and the parts played, first by the newspaper and then the various investigations, exploring the data, uncovering witnesses, facing problems posed by reconciling the accounts and the lapses of time before taking them, and the conflicting explanations that both structure the research and emerge out of it. In short, we find a machine that might come from science fiction, a technical-military setting and its associated personnel, and witnesses from the civilian world. We will follow up all these elements.

However, at this point – at the outset – I want to bring out the fundamental sense of instability one experiences when reading such a report.

[1] This summary of the Coyne incident is taken from Clark (1998: 114–119).

We begin with a description of an empirical object, but immediately are caught in questions of perception and apprehension. Can we believe what the witnesses say? Are they mistaken? What would we have seen, had we been present? We cannot say what we make of such an incident, for the real and the imaginary cannot be separated in this instance. We are dealing with both perception of the world and the properties of the mind simultaneously which, rather than posing clear alternatives, overlap and change back and forth. This is the quality that provides our starting point: flying saucers are marked by their ability to appear – become real – and disappear – turn into problems of thought – without resolution.

A first approach

Flying saucers then present us with a specific problem: their power to resist any settled scheme of explanation. Reports of flying saucer sightings have become commonplace since their first appearance in 1947, and the physical forms and properties described had been anticipated in science fiction for fifty years before that. The problem concerns the status we give these sightings and reports. We cannot start straightaway by turning to reports and analysing them, although that moment will come; we have first to discuss in broad terms the work they do and the load they carry.

There have been three common strategies adopted in response to reports. The first has been to classify these reports as true, claiming that what has been seen is real and needs further investigation. The second, that a mistake has been made, a misidentification, so that the report is wrong and the claim in error. The third is that the claims of sightings are evidence of acts of imagination. The three candidates are truth, error, and fiction. Yet each of these classifications fails to convince. In the first case, despite numerous cases and extensive debate about criteria, there is no uncontroverted evidence in favour of the existence of flying saucers of a sort that wholly resists sceptical handling. In the second, attempts to explain away such reports as mistaken perceptions fail to do justice to the testimonies and the integrity of the informants. The third option, that we are dealing in made-up stories subsequently taken to be true, falls by the same criterion as the second; witnesses should be granted some position beyond simply making it up or being unduly credulous. Each position has sufficient flaws to push the enquirer to the next; together, they form a circuit.

Moreover, the same fundamental attitude, that of taking seriously the actors and witnesses involved and allowing them practical experience, responsibility, intelligence and integrity at least equal to that of the enquirer, applies also to the critics and sceptics. They form part of the same circle but start from another position, that of assuming error or fiction as the initial point for their enquiry.

Rather than choose between these positions, we can begin by noticing that each demands both elaboration and concessions in order to work. Elaboration in this regard: everybody concerned knows how to handle the possibility of flying saucers, whether they subscribe to their existence or not, and knows what kind of behaviour may be expected of them. In essence, this behaviour comes down to that expected from 'unknown intentional forms of life' (Méheust 2007): it displays the characteristics of minds distinct from our own, but recognizable to us and in some sort of relation to us. Alien intelligence shows intention and the potential to communicate. Representations of flying saucers present a consistent set of ideas and expectations, one that has been sustained for seventy years and was anticipated before that; they are no passing social fad, and they observe rules.

And concession in this sense: even the most sceptical approaches, typically attributed to natural scientists, allow for the possibility – however thin – of such phenomena. The classification of reports always creates a residue of cases that cannot be explained by our present state of knowledge. And new evidence may appear; indeed, that possibility derives from the 'hard' sciences underlying the research of the size and extent of the universe and of the origins of life, and there have been programmes searching for evidence of patterned – and therefore intelligent – signals from non-human sources since the late 1950s. We might say that, although controversial, these reports seem to be allowed for even by the positions that most contest them.

In short, reports of flying saucers are widespread, long-lived and show recognizable properties. Yet, despite this ordinariness, longevity and consistency, they are also hard to make sense of; they provoke scandal.

The problem cannot therefore be reduced to two questions, 'true, or not?' and, if not, 'error, or fiction?' Instead, I propose that we take reports of flying saucer sightings as coming within what we might call the 'grammar of the possible', and so within our shared categories and classifications, keeping the rival claims of truth, error and fiction in the picture without deciding finally between them. Evidence will come first from the vigour with which the reports are advocated by some and simultaneously contested by others, and second from the amount of time and money expended on exploring and expounding those possibilities in various parts of our present society. We are looking at investments: we could consider the commitment made by people who make reports or who join small groups awaiting the imminent coming of flying saucers, as well as the commerce around the production and consumption of relevant popular science and science fiction, in print, films and now on-line, and these investments are matched and indeed exceeded by those parts of scientific, technological and defence research budgets which are justified to some extent by reference to the possibility of contacting civilizations on other planets or which are devoted to the search for extra-terrestrial intelligence.

The object of investigation is then the status given to reports of flying saucers. This may disappoint some readers, who wish the investigator to state a clear position: are we dealing with real things or with social conventions, with natural objects or cultural products? In practice, however, we are dealing in objects which share characteristics of both realms. These objects are simultaneously active and elusive: they produce effects in the world – not least the expenditure of time and transfers of money – and yet cannot be shown definitively even to exist. They consist in distributed effects and are therefore complex, and any representation of them is always problematic. In these characteristics, in their lacking simplicity and inadequacy of representations, they recall such practices familiar to anthropological study as divination, healing and spirit possession. At the same time, there are many advanced aspects of our society, technical, scientific and other, which are taken up and mirrored in these phenomena. Reports of flying saucers combine aspects of both, and by their insistence question the coherence of our understanding of the contemporary world.

Natural objects or social convention?

Let us look further at this mixed nature. What is lacking in the classification of statements into either true, or error, or fiction? At first sight, it works well. We can begin with the common-sense distinction between things that are produced, on the one hand, and, on the other, things that are found. There are two classes of object: the first is made by humans working together; it is the product of convention, we might say, of human agreement. The other is natural; real things that exist in the world, independent of human effort. The business of anthropologists, we could conclude, is to examine the products of conventions and that of scientists relates to natural objects.[2] These are different objects and demand different methods; you find a natural object such as a specific signal from space, a new species, or a previously unknown fossil, and work from there, but if you want to find out about flying saucers, the best thing you can do is seek out a group with the relevant interests and ask to join in their practices.

Studies of flying saucers over the last seventy years are marked by this opposition. On the one hand, you find claims that flying saucers are natural objects, that they are 'real' in the sense of being found; they are 'given' to the senses. There are then conflicts over the truth of these claims, in which frame the alternatives of error or fiction appear, to which we will return in a moment. On the other hand, it is possible to study the 'beliefs' of the group in question – their presuppositions and sources and practices (and parallel examples) – without any reference to the disputed reality of the objects. The argument goes as follows: social scientists know there are human groups which report contact with flying saucers, and which believe in their reality. But since the majority of social scientists do not subscribe to that belief, their initial conclusion is that claims concerning the existence of flying saucers have social meaning but do not stand up with respect to the reality of the objects seen. We then 'bracket out' objective truth claims and focus on collective practices, collective representations, and rhetorical

---

2   Note, however, that I will present a different account of the work of both natural scientists and anthropologists.

appeals made between parties concerning the persuasiveness or otherwise of different world views.

The difficulty with this second position concerns the judgement introduced by the social scientists: the decision that there is a class of behaviour where the actors are deceived or indifferent to truth and moreover, not open to enlightenment. While it is quite usual for people to make mistakes, to be taken in or to form a conclusion on insufficient information, in time they generally correct these views and repair the situation. Likewise, they can tell stories but, if questioned, may acknowledge their fictions as such. And, for this reason, the normal anthropological response to such an initial judgement – that the people in question are fundamentally mistaken in some regard – is to presume that more work is necessary on the social scientist's part; that the original apprehension was insufficient. For, in practice, one cannot separate out people's pragmatic behaviour – their working with what is given – and their beliefs, commitments and so forth, by referring to notions of incorrigible error. Yet in many cases, when confronted with anomalous beliefs close to home, we treat those beliefs as erroneous, supposing them to be a result of a range of factors such as a lack of education, cultural and economic isolation, and the survival of earlier beliefs now discarded in the wider society as superstition. In this fashion, social scientists become actors in the field under consideration: both the social scientists and their subjects make discriminations and offer evaluations, excluding some positions and identifying with others. In general, although not always, social scientists identify as sceptics.

The issue then is that the initial division between natural objects and social conventions and its handling in this case becomes part of the empirical materials under consideration, and social scientific studies often reproduce ways of thought we find 'on the ground'. Yet, a careful reading should seek something different to unconscious participation in the field of enquiry. A complicating factor in the instance of flying saucers lies in the fact that all parties – believers, sceptics and enquirers – are members of the same broad society and in many regards share the same resources, even if put to different ends. Indeed, each party simultaneously poses a challenge to the other modes of interpretation and yet performs complex strategies of borrowing and distorting elements from the other practices, ignoring some and highlighting other aspects of the rival productions. As evidence of this complex situation, as we have remarked, despite their presumed non-existence the notion of flying saucers nevertheless conveys a good deal of sense to everybody concerned: we have strong ideas about what they are and do and what is appropriate and inappropriate to claim about them. And, perhaps because of this detailed knowledge, we may also allow ourselves the thin possibility that they might exist; there is a distinct ambiguity about the status of flying saucers. This ambiguity is borne witness to by the energy of the arguments for and against their existence; these objects are not taken for granted but essentially contested, and that is part of their nature. The notion of flying saucers belongs to a group of ideas which we think we understand very well and yet, simultaneously, of which we find it hard to grasp the inner logic. It has a quality that demands investigation of another kind.

Errors and fictions

Since the existence of flying saucers is ambiguous, and the categories of the investigators are implicated as well as those of the subjects of the investigation, we can see that the question of how to classify these cultural products is also caught up as part of the material to be considered. The most helpful discussion I have found of the issues is by a philosopher, Tim Crane, who introduces the distinction between fiction and error in a discussion of what he calls 'non-existent objects of thought'.[3] On the one hand, such an object of thought may be an error, so that what has been accepted to be the case, even among a large group of people, turns out to be untrue. On the other hand, we may take it to be a fiction, for we can represent objects which do not exist; they can have names and properties, and we can make judgements about them. This process is common enough

---

[3] Crane's preferred term is non-existent intentional objects' (Crane 2013: 5), intentional because our thought is directed towards objects in acts of belief, memory, hope, fear and so forth, and non-existent because some of these objects of thought are not real.

with fictional characters; Crane mentions Sherlock Holmes, about whom we may speculate in detailed ways without imagining he existed. A key feature, Crane suggests, is that this talk of non-existent people and things is 'rooted in our talk and thought about the world' (Crane 2013: 14), so that non-existent objects are mapped for the most part in terms of known representations (cf. Crane 2013: 68–70). At the same time, we can make judgements about such objects, such as 'Sherlock Holmes is more famous than any living detective' (Crane 2013: 13).

The distinction between error and fiction reproduces that between natural facts and social convention: you can get your facts wrong or, under some circumstances, you can make up what you say, or sit lightly to the real state of affairs. One condition is real, the other imaginative, we might say, and the second is to a degree parasitic on the first, for it is improvised on the basis of existing representations and so cannot make much practical contribution and should not be relied on as a reliable basis for action. Despite this, Crane says little directly about error; for him, the exercise is one of bracketing out and simplifying: he can ignore time and change and set aside areas where categories overlap, for analysing issues of existence and non-existence need not be thought of as time-dependent, and areas of overlap are dealt with by a theory of metaphor whereby one speaks of one (fictional) thing in terms appropriate to another (which is real). Clarity, we might say, is bought at the price of freezing the frame and presenting fleeting products as stable elements from which a narrative can be constructed, isolated from their conditions of production, sustaining and disappearing.

Yet these concerns – of time dependency, overlapping categories, and appearance and disappearance – are of central importance for the social scientist, for whom categories are not clear and distinct but mixed, and many of whose concepts are found to operate under certain circumstances but not under others. In this perspective, time and change are everything. If we take the figure of Sherlock Holmes as an example, he could not have appeared before the 1880s because he embodies positivist presuppositions which were only formed at that time. Holmes (or his author and readers) assumes a single, rule-governed universe in which every action has its reason, a reason that can be discerned by an informed, dispassionate mind and a trained eye, and so it is possible to reconstruct the behaviour of the criminal, tracing the sequence of his thoughts as he adapts rational means to his dishonest ends in an efficient manner. If you discover the criminal's motive, you have explained everything. This is Holmes' charm for the reader, along with his celebration of the new means of communication available – the newspaper advertisement columns, the railway, the telegram. Without this economy of means and ends in an ordered world, with proportionate effort expended in the pursuit of his desires, it would be impossible either to understand the criminal's actions or to anticipate his next move. As it is, criminal and detective share a common world and a common model of action, neither of which has any place for contingency or inefficiency, for mistakes, misapprehensions, or misunderstandings.

Yet this is in many regards a short-lived model; this position no longer holds in its entirety by the 1920s. There is testimony to this in John Buchan's *The Three Hostages* (1924), where another fictitious character demolishes the possibility of rational deduction of the Holmesian kind being effective in the modern world. After the recent War, this character says, people no longer argue or behave rationally. Under these circumstances, where you cannot take anything for granted, the detective story cannot work; 'the facts are no longer sober' (Buchan 1966: 13), and a new kind of literature is called for. This literature will deal with the properties of the mind which come to the surface in the new world condition. With the breakdown of civilized order, pragmatic reason can no longer be relied on; instead, we look to the power of the unconscious memory to make connections and, as the novel makes clear, previously hidden forces emerge, not only those of anarchy and mischief on the public stage, but also hypnotism and mind control on the personal level, the ability to implant subconscious instruction and to cause forgetfulness, and the possibility of making a second personality come out from beneath the first, conscious self. We are offered a picture both of a world masked by deceits and lies, propaganda and mass persuasion, and of individual lives marked by significant coincidences, synchronicities and occult powers. In short, in place of an 1890s world marked by perception and physical action, linked by the conscious weighing of clear impressions, followed by evaluation and decision, we have a 1920s world in which mental phenomena predominate, with overlapping categories and loosened causal links.

This contrast between two moments is only captured in fictional form and should not be taken too seriously as social analysis, but it points to a distinctive sociological concern. We are confronted here with shifts in presuppositions, and so with making connections between topics which are often kept separate. In this instance, the topics are, first, a shift in political, social, and intellectual order and, second, individual experience, the possibilities of human action and interaction, virtuous behaviour and delinquency, under these conditions. The crux is that, at certain points and under certain conditions, organizing categories break down and new forms emerge and that, under these particular conditions, anomalous objects – fictions – may appear with peculiar properties and powers which cannot be easily represented.

We may add a further point: the existing forms of representation, including the divide between found objects and manufactured conventions, which attempt to map these singular conditions will inevitably miss a good deal of what is happening, although the different accounts will retain aspects of their properties and effectiveness. We are concerned, then, on the one hand, with the collapse and reformulation of categories and, on the other hand, with the impotence of established forms of representation to do justice to these singular events. It is to these kinds of issue that the appearance of flying saucers directs our attention in a later period: reports of flying saucers draw into sight the mutability of the presuppositions which we bring to bear in allowing the world to make sense.

The object of investigation

In short, we have taken four steps to identify the object of the investigation. It is characterized, first, by an alternation between real and imaginary phases: it does not take a stable, fixed form. Then, because of this fluidity, it cannot be captured by any of the conventional forms of representation, and, as evidence of this impossibility, each of these forms – truth, error, fiction – borrows some features from its rivals and concedes ground on other aspects. From this it follows, third, that the categories of investigation are implicated in grasping the object and, just as it changes form, so do they, and we are required to go beyond the alternatives of a naturalistic or, on the other hand, a cultural approach. And last, if the object of study is composed both by the appearance of new things and a simultaneous alteration in the presuppositions within which they can be perceived and made sense of, our only recourse can be to specific examples, to case studies (reports) set in a particular time and context, in order that we might observe in process both the emergence of new objects (records of sightings) and signs of shifts in the categories at work, often signaled by new terms or incoherence in narratives.

This combination of a shift in framework and appearance of a new thing is our object. In the remainder of this chapter, I will outline the approach adopted to describe such an object before, in the next, offering a sketch of the context in which it first came to light.

II. Approach

Our object is then a complex one; even a simple example such as the Coyne incident calls attention to the involvement of a number of separate areas and scales of activity, the overlap of these usually distinct topics, and the transitory nature of these interactions. We might think of the appearance of 'non-existent objects of thought' (considered in a different optic to that a philosopher might bring to bear) as marking 'events': moments when both things on the ground change and the terms in which they are grasped shift, so that both what is given and what is thought alter simultaneously. We are thinking about the emergence of the new, of novelty, when established forms of representation no longer serve.

To spell out the issues again, because they are central to the argument: in the first place, if we focus on the dynamic aspect of mutations in social space, these changes implicate not simply categories of thought and the negotiation of new claims, but the simultaneous alterations of real boundaries, creating new parties and new kinds of evidence. It is not the case that new concepts allow the re-description of previously existing but hitherto unrecognized phenomena, which are unveiled by an advance in understanding. Rather, all the elements – participants, categories and meanings, claims and evidence, and their institutional setting – emerge as parts of a simultaneous 'event'. No part of the social order is left unaffected. And, in the second place, any strictly contemporary attempt to represent these complex events will necessarily fail to grasp fully what is going on or what has happened, in part because of the alteration in the categories by which the change is apprehended. There is a distinction to be made between the creation of new values and the recognition of established values.

Such problems recur in social life. My suggestion is that the appearance of flying saucers is such an event and that each later sighting bears at least echoes of the initial disruption. It involves the application of human intelligence in a situation defined by a shift in social space, a shift in which terms, boundaries, activities, and roles are all reformulated. We are not concerned with an essence, nor with sorting truth from error, nor with invention, but with a series of responses to new circumstances and opportunities, displayed in a proliferation of forms. Under these conditions, new phenomena and behaviour appear; to put matters briefly, the collective human imagination can produce objects of thought which have practical – material – effects, effects which belong to no one party. How do we approach such an object?

Lesson from an earlier study: Three components

Who are the main players and what are the stakes in the case of reports of flying saucers? On the face of it, there are three broad forms of human activity involved. We noticed these forms when considering the Coyne incident, but they can be drawn out further, again by using a specific example.

There is, first, a series of sightings, events concerning space craft, flying saucers or unidentified flying objects. To give a specific, classic instance, Festinger and his colleagues studied a group in the Chicago area in the early 1950s who had been contacted by non-human intelligent life forms and who expected the imminent arrival of flying saucers (Festinger et al.

2008). Festinger gives an account of a sequence of events[4] produced on the ground by interactions between three parties: a group receiving messages from non-human others through a series of spirit mediums, the investigating social scientists, who had infiltrated the group, and an audience comprising of local people and a number of social organizations including the press. I have published a re-reading of Festinger on which I draw here (Jenkins 2013): the key to the year-long episode consisted in the presuppositions the first two parties brought to bear and, in particular, the powers each attributed to language. For while the social scientists believed language to be, ideally, a transparent and inert medium for representing reality, the group on the contrary held words to possess a creative power and to effect real changes; they were therefore more cautious and discriminating concerning the messages received, what the recipients of the messages reported, and with whom they communicated the contents. Owing to these different presuppositions, a series of misunderstandings resulted which may be summed up as, on the part of the investigators, refutation of any claim as to the existence of flying saucers but, in the perspective of the group, success in responding to the messages, so averting a global catastrophe: they achieved their ends and fulfilled their vocation under chaotic conditions.

This short-lived series of events constitutes one level of engagement with unknown intentional life forms and considered by itself it has its own in-built complexities, constructed around the interplay between recipients of messages and sightings and investigators of their reports, played out in front of a local audience and amplified by the press. However, there were also two other forms of human activity involved in the picture, forms with different institutional settings and distinct timelines.

In the Chicago case, beyond the level of the events described, there was also a series of overlapping informal social groups implicated. There were those involved in sightings of flying saucers, since their first appearance in 1947, which included the principal medium's right-hand man;

---

4   We shall have to use 'event' in two ways, to denote a singularity of the kind outlined in the previous paragraphs, event in a strong sense, and, as here, event in a non-technical sense, to remark a series of things that happen one after another. The context should make clear which sense we intend.

these witnesses and, a bit later, 'contactees', formed a loose network which included some right-wing activists. Then, there were suburban flying saucer clubs and a wider series of metaphysical discussion groups, including the recent innovations of Dianetics and Scientology. These produced their own news sheets and magazines and listened to the witnesses and contactees. And last, there was an extensive production of science fiction publications and films which both shaped the categories and styles of argument of the narrowly focussed groups and disseminated them. Festinger's account presents some evidence of these groups' activities and cites some of the literature produced by groups but does not investigate the role of either science fiction or film.

Further to this loose milieu, there was a quite distinct sector, more institutionalized and better funded, and close to the state; we might call this a 'constellation of technical interests'.[5] This constellation included government departments, the armed forces, manufacturing companies, and departments of research in industry and universities, comprising a series of interlocking institutions, sources of finance and intellectual projects, projects such as the early phases of Information Technology, communications, and space flight. This constellation is effectively absent from Festinger's account.

Despite great differences in scale, approach and motivation, this constellation of interests was not entirely separable from the concerns of the informal milieus, from which the Chicago group sprang. The three social forms – the constellation of technical interests, the informal overlapping milieus, and the year-long series of events – were largely independent, existing and developing in different time frames, and yet they also impinged on one another. Clearly, technological and scientific advances provided material for the small group's imagination, often mediated by the informal milieus. But there is evidence too that the constellation also responded to the inventions of these informal milieus, both in the contemporary creation of an Air Force unit collecting reports on flying saucers and, the most striking instance, the programme termed the Search for Extra Terrestrial

---

5 The phrase is borrowed from a seminar given by Caroline Humphrey in Cambridge, 17 October 2015.

Intelligence (SETI), inaugurated in the late 1950s and, although formally discontinued in 1993, pursued by other means since then to the present.

In short, I wish to draw attention to the dispersed nature of the organizing categories and ideas involved in reports of flying saucers, for they emerge from a complex institutional, intellectual, and personal setting. As the Coyne incident indicates, we cannot fully separate the sequences of incidents and reports, the work of the informal milieu and anticipations in science fiction, and the technical constellation with its organizing role in military and scientific technology and in space research.

Approach adopted in this essay

Although I have introduced these three elements in the order of priority we normally give them when starting from reports, I shall present them in a different sequence, for this will allow some different emphases to appear. The commonly held picture is, in the first place, there is a public that is concerned with sightings and testimonies. Then, there is a constellation of military, technical and industrial interests that play a role in the first group's reports, largely through the borrowing of details of innovations, but which appear to have little to do with those stories in reality. And last, there is the science fiction milieu, the world of writers, publishers and readers, which draw features of both the other two strands into a single narrative.

As a first step, I pay attention to the chronological order and dates of the documents used. By taking this chronological approach, trying to limit anticipation of later formulations and their projection back, I have had to revise the order of development demanded by the common-sense picture. The crucial element is the military-technical constellation; images of 'life elsewhere' took on a different form due to the extraordinary technical innovations associated with the Second World War. More, the development of ideas of life elsewhere fell to the United States Air Force in this immediate Post-War period. The form in which life elsewhere was conceived was the product of an organization using the latest advanced technology in a situation of a high state of threat to home security, the early

Cold War. This is not, of course, a new claim. The important point is that ideas concerning the contemporary forms of life from beyond this planet cannot be separated out from the constellation of military, technological and industrial interests, nor from the products of 'Big Science', that is, from advanced technologies cooperatively produced by universities, corporations and the armed forces and funded by the tax base, and so of interest both to politicians and the press. Flying saucers were not produced nor discerned by small, informal social groups; the primary work was done, and the forms given shape and substance, in this central context and primarily by a unit set up in Air Force intelligence. This work of production is the subject of the last chapter, which presents a key to the argument.

But before looking at this production, we have to consider another factor. That is the broad frame which allowed the conception of novelty in terms of new technology, if we accept that flying saucers were conceived in a world dominated by and in part constructed through means of communication developed in warfare. This is the subject of the second chapter. In this fashion, we look first at changes in categories peculiar to the period and its conditions and then at the specific history of new appearances; together, mutations in social space and, simultaneously, the creation of new conditions and actors.

In Chapter 2, therefore, we consider the context in which sightings of flying saucers emerged. The double object identified – the combination of a new kind of object and a new way of seeing – appeared in the aftermath of the Second World War, in which new kinds of military technology and new types of media had been developed and had mutually formed one another. This post-War period may be described in terms of the intimate connection of technology and media, the fragmented nature of experience and the new relations to time that accompanied it, and the attitude of mind, concerned with deciphering hidden connections and motives, which became appropriate to living in such an environment. All these features – technological innovation, the development of new media, and the impulse of warfare, together with new powers of perception – are characteristic of the history of flying saucers. In order to grasp the implications of these innovations from the perspective of personal experience, I explore these contemporary features in a second section through an early example, a Latin American science fiction tale from 1940.

And, in Chapter 3, we ask how, then, do these possibilities 'hatch'? This chapter traces in detail the emergence of the 'interplanetary hypothesis' in US Air Force circles. We follow the stages of realization of the idea of flying saucers in the context of the developing Cold War, outlining an environment structured by the invention and monitoring of new technologies and driven by acute security concerns, heightened by the outbreak of the Korean War. This is the story of a piece of intelligence work, an investigation using scientific methods within a setting defined by a long experience of warfare. Our main source is the only contemporary account produced by one of the actors – a book which played its part in the condensation of the properties attributed to UFOs – supplemented by documents released later under freedom of information requests and taking the debates they have provoked into consideration. There are two strands to the narrative. On the one hand, an account of the development of a scientific hypothesis, a progressive identification and conceptualization of the 'UFO' through a process of observation and investigation, which lent substance to popular ideas of flying saucers. On the other hand, the theme of mounting internal opposition to the hypothesis, not on scientific grounds but for pragmatic reasons, focussing on the disruptive effects experienced with the reception of the popular idea, leading to the curtailing of the scientific investigation. Together, these two strands comprise the original image of the flying saucer, made up of indications of serious scientific engagement with the problem and, equally, evidence of an official desire to disengage from this research and quash public interest in the topic. This constitutes an enduring pattern.

Further developments

This first essay then answers two questions: in the first place, under what circumstances do images of flying saucers appear, and then, where and how are these images hatched? Together, these form a coherent subject matter. But further questions arise in trying to gain a thorough understanding of the topic and these are the subject of the following essays in the series. It is worth indicating at this point the overall plan of development and the nature of the wider argument to which they each contribute.

The second essay is concerned with the seed which took hold in the circumstances described and which gained form and substance in the post-War period. This seed was composed in the science fiction milieu, and it carried with it some specific properties, characteristics which play out in the subsequent history. The crucial characteristics which fitted with the preoccupations of intelligence work in the period concern the idea of intelligent beings coming from elsewhere and monitoring human activity in a detailed fashion, alert particularly to advances in human industries and technology and the production of ever-more destructive weaponry, and able as well to tune into human mental processes and their moral dilemmas. These distinctive features have a particular origin: they were created by the theosophical synthesis first elaborated in the 1880s and transmitted through pulp science fiction stories, with accounts of non-human life forms travelling between planets and engaging with modern human lives, generally for the purpose of our enlightenment, and they have run through the subsequent history of flying saucer sightings. The second essay is therefore given over to reading a particular story from 1940s pulp magazines, famous in the local history of flying saucers, and to spelling out the contribution Theosophy makes, a contribution which then feeds into the world of technical developments and security problems which are explored in the first essay.

In this fashion, we offer in this first essay an account of the 'lens' shaping the images and of the production of flying saucers in the heart of the constellation of technical interests making up a central part of modern society and, in the second, of the seeding of the original idea. It is possible after that to trace the continuing life of the image created, noting how, as the Air Force sought to rid itself of any further engagement with rumours of alien spacecraft, the newly developed space industry sought evidence of signals from other, non-human civilizations as part of its spectrum of activities. This is the business of the third essay, which focusses on a concern with models of communication and their limits as an organizing theme.

Neither the thesis of the Cold War origins of flying saucers nor that of the importance of theosophical ideas to the characteristics of extra-terrestrial life is original, though I hope to have worked through both with a certain thoroughness. But put together, they free us to consider the last element in the mix identified in this introductory chapter: ordinary human lives and their responses to flying saucers in terms of sightings and testimonies. The wider considerations allow us to see what features are taken for granted, which go without saying on the part of all parties, and which prove controversial and cannot be resolved. And by laying out a spectrum of positions, it is possible to discern an underlying logic to the informants' accounts, and it is here that my principal contribution lies. In the second trio of essays, we look at the uses to which a range of civilians put these newly appeared phenomena and how those uses develop. The aim is to create an anthropological account of the lives of ordinary people who have recourse to reports of flying saucers and their occupants.

This approach is to step away from a widespread style of earlier academic writing about flying saucer reports which conjures away the wider intellectual and institutional setting, largely ignoring both the traditions being drawn on and the nature of education in those traditions, and also neglecting the work these claims perform by joining times and places, creating new resources, relationships and potential for action, and distinguishing people from their neighbours. By focussing solely on sightings and the life of the groups making these claims, this rejected perspective reproduces the exclusions and focus of the actors themselves, who speak largely of exceptional experience and neglect all reference to the social construction of the possibility of contact, the collective and transmitted nature of these constructions, and the human work the alien visitors allow them to achieve. This taking-over of perspective from the indigenous self-presentation means the social scientists tend to repeat the question asked by many outside investigators: are we dealing in scientific facts – do we accept these claims of exceptional experience at face value – or are the informants psychologically deceived?[6]

---

6   There is also a series of social scientific accounts which place reports and events in a wider social, institutional, political and intellectual setting and I draw on these at appropriate points.

I have therefore taken a series of civilian examples – ones well known in the history of flying saucers – to explore questions of construction and context, the traditions drawn on, the apprenticeships served, and the uses to which the new phenomena are put, what they allow to be brought together and what put apart. The uses are, of course, many; they are not all of one kind, but certain patterns appear to be constant, shaped indeed by the original properties set by the theosophical groundwork, defining what is characteristic and what is not for flying saucers. We follow these changes through the next two essays (the fourth and fifth in the series), exploring the life of flying saucers and their successor forms once they got out of the crucible of their making in the world of Cold War security.

In the first of these, I review the typical forms that emerge relating to claims of objective truth and denial of the same, on the one hand, and the work of the imagination, on the other, through considering two case studies. The first takes an early debate between an advocate of the reality of flying saucers, drawing on evidence from Air Force reports, and his opponent, a scientific sceptic who explained all reports away as the mistaken apprehension of natural phenomena. This debate set the broad terms in which later discussions shared. The second case study describes the life and work of a person whose career became shaped around the idea of contact with flying saucers, and who displays the social dynamics experienced around the claims and counterclaims associated more generally with sightings and reports. These two cases demonstrate in detail the construction of the field of possible interpretations, the 'grammar' of flying saucer reports outside the military-technical sphere.

And the fifth essay explores a wider set of encounters with flying saucers by members of the public from around the United States in the next decades. In this study, I use reports by three journalists who were sympathetic to the individual claims and who took the informants seriously; each transformed the quality of reporting of sightings, and their writings take us from sightings at a distance to ever-closer encounters, ending with cases of abduction and abduction becoming a widely employed metaphor for certain kinds of common experience. Significant features in these encounters repeat elements found in the military records: we find the disruption of lives and new connections made, links established joining distinct times, adjustments in resources and initiative available to the witness, and the inflexion of life paths. The important facts are all to one side of questions about technology and possibility, although these questions may be the currency in which claims are made.

All the essays, taken together, present a wide spectrum of styles of encounter with life forms from elsewhere and allow us to identify the range of presuppositions which underwrite the different possibilities they contain. In considering abductions, we encounter a third organizing theme beyond those of technological innovation and the communication of information: the business of memory and the recovery of past events. Through the various case studies, we can see how, under particular conditions, as the explanatory frame alters, imaginary objects simultaneously cease to be expressions of realistic descriptions and become active. Under certain conditions both of circumstance and interpretation, virtual objects can produce effects in the world; they become real.

Tracing the ground rules of this repeated shift between real and virtual conditions is the business of the sixth essay. In each essay, the empirical and historical descriptions are interspersed with more abstract reflection, the purpose of which is to find concepts that allow us to make better sense of the materials we have been reading in terms that do not crush or distort the concerns expressed in the reports and writings. The last essay is concerned to extend this reflection on the empirical materials. If the first three essays focus on the range of behaviour and styles of thought that can emerge even within the apparently sober genre of realist description, the last one describes the characteristics of a different style of thinking that emerges once conditions neutralize the plausibility of a realist account. In this way, we identify the anomalous characteristics found in the empirical materials, characteristics that allow the resolution of various problems, in particular, the role of unprovable ideas in the generation of scientific insight, on the one hand, and the resistance of non-standard or exceptional episodes to reductive sociological explanation, on the other. This essay concludes with a summary and review of the argument and offers some general observations.

Discussion

The three topics from which we start, the science fiction milieu, technical and military circles, and anomalous events pertaining to ordinary lives, concern different kinds of collective groups. They operate at different scales and display different kinds of social relations, although some common patterns emerge; they work with different kinds of resources and means of communication, and they demand distinct styles of research. Science fiction is the subject of what we might call 'subterranean' literary studies, the cultural studies end of that discipline. The constellation of state, technical and commercial interests requires a focus on the dynamics of big organizations, the history of the sciences, technology and communications studies, and some military intelligence history. And concern with reports made by members of the public lends itself to ethnographic approaches and the reading of testimonies. Yet, while the three groups appear on the surface to have little to do with one another, they make contributions at various points to one another in the detail of each story. While it is impossible to be competent in all these areas, nevertheless they have to be brought into relation in order to pursue the object of research.

For the value of these detailed moments of contact – moments of lending, borrowing, influence, change of direction – is they allow us to grasp our subject matter, the shifts in categories and boundaries which are quickly covered over in retrospect and not fully grasped at the time. By tracing aspects of the empirical sequence of things happening, claims made, disputes fought out and so forth, we can discern another history, that of the 'event' in the more technical sense. These transfers and borrowings happen at times when matters of calibration, measuring and ordering become confused, when there is a momentary hesitation in the means by which we make sense of change, moments which are transitory and yet repeated. I aim to give a description of the processes at work in these moments when thought and feeling change and new objects such as flying saucers make their appearance. These processes are a prime anthropological topic, the innovative force of collective ideas that can only appear through specific material instances.

We may remark that, in exploring the conditions allowing anomalous appearances, while we start with reliance on straightforward questions of chronology and sequence, we come to adopt a more nuanced account of time: the materials impose it. Nonetheless, chronology remains our starting point and principal guide. And likewise, if we end with the trio of technological innovation, the communication of information, and the vagaries of memory, passing by a range of non-standard concerns such as action at a distance, the life of spirits, and interplanetary travel, we can begin from a set of relatively solid concerns, dealing in science fiction, military weapons and communication systems, and reports of sightings. That is where we start, by considering how technology shapes everyday thought.

An endnote on reading and sources

Given the wide range of materials to be considered, it is worth making clear the approach adopted, to avoid any misunderstanding of the claims I am making. First, the subject matter, which is materials concerning reports. There is a relatively tight body of primary literature: there are reports of the first sightings, referred to as the 'classics', and then a series of later encounters. These are written up in a restricted number of early books that together influenced the development of the field, its terms and theories. There is also a much larger body of secondary materials, small-scale journal articles, books produced for commercial ends, television programmes and Internet debates, from the earliest days to the present, which recycle this finite body of sightings, reports, and formative discussions. This work of recycling, however, is both aided and made more complicated as contemporary official records become declassified and enter the public realm, allowing revision of the histories at issue: the distinction between primary and secondary is by no means easy to sustain fully.

I have confined myself to examples drawn from this first corpus, focussing on the core texts, exploring the interplay between them in terms of echoes, borrowings and shared or disputed solutions, while paying attention to the development of the field, including revisions of its vocabulary and theories, noting the language used and the models being imported.

In this fashion, we seek in the documents to discern traces of two chains of events, first, the stimuli being perceived and, second, their reporting. They are, of course, in practice mutually implicated.

This approach then distinguishes in principle between sightings and reports and concerns itself with what lies between them. This follows from the description of the Coyne incident. The crucial question is why this sequence was counted as an 'incident'; why an unexplained sighting took on significance and was construed as an encounter with an unidentified, intentionally controlled, craft. The investigation is organized by the dissonance between the two moments of sighting and report. The phenomenon of flying saucers is created in the space between these two kinds, perception and image, styles of emergence, on the one hand, and reception, on the other, and the purpose of this series of essays is to trace the creation and development of this space. We might ask three questions: where do these 'fictitious' forms come from? How are they hatched – how do they become reports? And what happens once they are created, when fictions become real with independent lives? Cases – incidents – although appearing to come first, in practice repeat and make clear a process of production, which we may call the 'power of the false', understood as a technical, not a moral, matter: the definition and construction of flying saucers through the non-correspondence of sightings and reports.

This series of essays, then, is largely a study of reports in this perspective, and the reports will be familiar to anybody who knows the field. It is not meant as an exhaustive account of the core literature, nor a survey of the wider materials; instead, it is a process of re-reading, an exercise in defamiliarization, reading well-known texts in some detail to discern the moments when both objects and categories shift in form. In short, by slow reading, one can trace the emergence of the object under construction. In the course of reading in this perspective, certain writings gain authority, usually because of their qualities of thought and engagement. Within these writings, we – reading together – can see how certain incidents have been handled and how, over time, they build up a series of interpretations of the flying saucer problem, and how the style of interpretation has altered over time. It is possible to identify key sources and to describe how the overall discussion both arose and developed or, at least, to discern some pattern in the flow. I am in this fashion offering a 'genealogy', tracing the formation and development of an idea through a close reading of a limited body of texts, a reading that allows us to see the resources, with their limits and compulsions, which are brought to bear in many different circumstances to make sense of various anomalies that emerge through various incidents of post-War life, and which continue to operate to the present. This approach, then, does not aim at comprehensive cover but at developing a form of comprehension.

Certain aspects follow from the focus on reading conceived in this fashion.

First, the importance of detail; I take the view that only the exhaustive can be truly interesting. We start from moments in the lives of individuals and small groups, with the experience of encounters, when shifts in personal lives match with wider alterations in possibility and definition. We begin, then, from empirical materials and sequences conceived in linear time and watch as more abstract ideas emerge from the materials and sequences, as questions of social structure and issues about the complex nature of time appear and, in turn, transform back into 'real life'.

Second, this approach begins then from the human scale of experience, of making sense, and sense of mutability, in order to raise more general questions of social structure and continuity. Because the subject matter concerns the transformation of both things on the ground and in apprehension, so that categories and empirical materials transform and play one into the other, we have to pay attention to specific texts and the rationale that can be traced in them. The focus on texts allows us to give the evidence for each claim and to test the ground for each abstraction. Other kinds of social science work with other kinds of material. If we were to move prematurely to a synthesis, it would be impossible to tell apart what emerges from the materials and the unexamined presuppositions brought to bear on those materials. Often, too, the unexamined presuppositions are carried over from or confirmed by one of the several positions present in the evidence. For these reasons, I have adopted a slow, reiterative approach, which we might call 'commentary'. First, I offer an initial description or reading. Then, ask what in this description catches the eye or demands further thought? Next, what do these episodes remind us of? From where do their models and resources derive? These are questions of context and local history. And last, what wider comparisons may be made, and which theoretical debates might assist our thinking? This includes: which parts of this intellectual history were being invoked in the earlier investigations, and how do we now construe them? Although these distinct elements may appear in a different order, the research begins always from the particular, from specific episodes, and the derivation of any more general observations may be traced and so justified from this sequence. In short, I have adopted a social anthropological and historical approach from the repertoire of the social sciences, and this is demanded by the particular object of study.

In the course of reading, I also have recourse to other writings to help give shape to the argument; these appear in their place.

Third, two kinds of material appear to be particularly favoured by actors in both the military technical world and the more informal interactions of civilians (which are the focus of the earlier and the later essays respectively), used to make intellectual sense and to engage with the phenomena in question: science fiction on the one hand and spiritualist séances and comparable 'occult' instances on the other. And these materials also help us analyse and understand what may be called the mechanisms at work at the human scale producing the effects with which we are concerned. In particular, they show how real and imaginary elements may be brought into a common space, juxtaposed, and exchanged, giving a sense of how the persistent characteristics of flying saucers may be sustained and made lively in different contexts.

Last, because of the focus on contemporary materials, the accounts given have to adopt something of their concerns and omissions. In particular, the accounts drawn from the early materials, before 1960, are exclusively in the male voice. Women's voices emerged only with the turn to abductions (though women's voices were present in the earlier materials as mediums but were ignored in contemporary studies – see Jenkins 2013). This emergence relates to a wider transformation being traced, the failure of realism as a self-sufficient idiom and the emergence of more reflective and multiple voices. The exclusively masculine tone of discussion of the early period is in keeping with its time.

In short, the strategy of attentive reading adopted is in accordance with the complex object at issue. If social science is not metaphysics but the gradual appreciation of what we may call partisan worldviews and their interactions, then presenting a case study will mean describing successively views which we will not adopt as our own but will supplement while, at the same time, appreciating their positive value as forms of life. Two things follow. It is relatively easy to be misread as an advocate of any one of the positions described. And we do not end up with the 'right' answer – a new metaphysical account – but rather with a series of corrections – supplements – and new perspectives. This is the only way to avoid a history celebrating progress without collapsing into cynicism or relativism concerning non-progressive elements. How else can we do justice to the extraordinary innovation and creation of new knowledge and successful technique found in the development of new defence technologies and, later, of space exploration, without giving the illusion of predestination on the one hand and leaving behind an age of superstition on the other? The answer lies in the ambition to do justice to all positions: in particular, by seeing the role that what at a later stage may be defined as 'error' or 'fiction' plays in the creation of new thought, and noting its recurrence, as such motifs play new roles in later engagements and new situations. Flying saucers allow us to construe wider aspects of the workings of a complex modern society: how such a society in its different parts 'thinks', establishes values and priorities, relates to technology, and reasons about human ills and well-being.

CHAPTER 2

Technology and the categories of experience

To sum up the argument of the first chapter in a paragraph: flying saucer reports constitute a puzzle as part of the contemporary world. By and large, we try to ignore the puzzle and look past the phenomena associated with them, but if we focus on them, the widespread nature of the reports and the reliable character of many of the witnesses demand some effort to comprehend them going beyond the partisan commitments of advocates and the persistent controversies that accompany the reception of the reports. Understanding the reports will involve grasping the simultaneous development of the objects in question and of the categories of apprehension; neither is independent of the other, and it is this joint history which is at issue.

The first question to emerge is what kind of thinking allows the problem to be put in this fashion, and when did it come into existence? What allows us to think in terms of flying saucers and their possibility or impossibility? We are concerned with the appearance of modern forms of the imagination, and the crux lies in changes associated with new forms of media. Or to be more exact, it lies in the link between technology and the media and the evolving relation between the two in the modern period.[1]

To put the argument in summary – it will be explored in more detail – a series of new technologies, dating from the end of the nineteenth century and extending to the present, have permitted new experiences and new forms of imagination. The gramophone, for example, allowed the experience of being addressed directly by an absent person, even a dead person. Radio, a later development, though not by much, permitted us to

---

[1] This has been a topic of discussion at least since Benjamin's essay 'The Work of Art in the Age of Mechanical Reproduction', first published in 1936 (Benjamin 2015).

hear disembodied voices from far away. Both, initially, had an uncanny quality; they abolished differences of time and space. Photographs, likewise, made present images of elsewhere, never encountered in experience, or brought before us images of people we may have known, even loved, but who had lives in other places. And motion pictures multiplied novelties of these kinds: they not only present records of stretches of other times and places, but – through recording and replaying – create new perspectives and new angles on scenes, not only allowing new things to be seen but fresh details to emerge, reframing incidents, calling attention to hitherto unperceived moments of significance, and presenting short sequences that may alter the meaning of an encounter. In short, we might say that new media created new kinds of experience and possibilities and turned our lives into new sorts of narrative.

New media have always had this kind of effect. But the means of recording, storage and replaying developed from the 1880s on were particularly striking both in their effects and in the widespread nature of their impact, touching not simply an elite few, but almost everyone, through radio and cinema, altering the nature of experience and memory, creating new shared ways of being in the world. As a population, we came to perceive everyday life in categories that derived from these experiences, these vivid enactments of things that are not there. The world in which we live has changed, and these new ways of grasping life as it is lived operate at several levels. For instance, we anticipate the sudden presence of minds from elsewhere; we can receive direct communication from absent friends; we can conceive of new perspectives on situations, modelled often on shots from above that reveal patterns of behaviour or shots from below that reveal relations of power, and, most of all, we can conceive of ourselves as caught up in stories, or being touched by other stories, unknown to us but going on in the same space. Our life is, to a degree, cinematic, shaped by audio-visual images. And once collectively we have glimpsed the power of media in this regard, we can conceive of the world as being ordered by codes and can imagine it is constructed by invisible means and controlled by unknown people whose intentions are hidden from us. A world shaped by experience of film is also, potentially, a paranoid world.

Flying saucers are a small feature of the imaginative space created within these new technological frames. They can be dated quite precisely: spaceships appeared in fiction contemporary with the development of radio and, like radio waves, travel through space, hiding their origin. The motives behind the appearance of spaceships are also often hidden – they make unexpected contact and convey messages with implications that are hard to evaluate. These ideas were elaborated in early science fiction, a branch of pulp publishing popularized in the first half of the twentieth century, which drew on theosophical speculations for many of its details, describing spirit forms travelling between planets, organizing cosmic evolution, and aiding the development of the human race.[2] These works offered a meditation on the contemporary human condition, confronted with the expansion of scientific knowledge and of the technology that accompanied it, and laid down most of the ground rules that apply in modern UFO sightings. In this fashion, science fiction provided content for a form arising independently.

But this is only to set the scene. We shall look first at the specific moment and context in which sightings of flying saucers emerged, identifying a range of characteristics that will serve in the analysis of reports, and then turn to a contemporary work of fiction which sought to explore the experience of encountering this new world condition.

I. Weapons and communication

We can offer a fairly precise date for the beginning of our puzzle. The history of human exploration of the possibility of life beyond the earth emerged at the end of the Second World War (1945). Although there had been interest expressed in such possibilities before this date (expressions that will play a part in this account), exploration only became a realistic option with the extraordinary developments in a whole range of technologies during and under the impulse of the War: not only rocket flight,

---

2   A claim I shall substantiate in the second essay, *Religion and Science Fiction*.

rocket guidance systems and radar, and the creation of new materials and fuel systems, but also the construction of new forms of handling information, notably in the development of the computer, together with advances in the recording, storage and transmission of a variety of wavelengths, allowing the manipulation and analysis of sound and images. This history, exploiting these options created during the conflict, has continued to the present.

The crucial point is that radical innovation in defence technologies has brought with it fundamental alterations in civilian media, so that the 'communication of information' became a central aspect of social life, creating a new role for modern media that we have come to take for granted. There is a double change, extraordinary technical innovation combined with a mutation in the categories by which we collectively apprehend everyday life, and the two faces cannot be prised apart. The principal symptoms of this close relationship between developments in technology and changes in the forms of media that accompany those developments are, on the one hand, a complex experience of time that emerges under these conditions and, on the other, a series of appropriate human attitudes and behaviour in response to this experience. In short, there is an alteration around the period of the Second War in what is the case (material conditions), how we know what the case is, and an appropriate ethical response: technological invention, travelling back and forth in time, and – as we shall see – paranoia. All three themes are integral to the world in which flying saucers made their appearance.

This perspective, concerning the development of technologies and, in particular, technologies concerned with handling information, has been explored in a series of essays by a media theorist, Friedrich Kittler, to whom we turn as a guide. For he has identified the series of themes which recur in investigating reports of sightings and which form part of the argument: a focus on Kittler's ideas allows us to glimpse the framework underlying the problem of flying saucers.

Kittler's overall thesis concerns a long time span: he suggests that around the 1880s an essentially literary model of apprehending the world, developed through the novel and poetry in the early part of the nineteenth century, was disrupted by the development of three new technologies for handling different kinds of information. In the first place, there was the recording and broadcasting of sound waves, embodied in the gramophone and subsequently in radio; in the second, the capturing and reproduction of visible light, initially through photography and later film; and third, the handling of written symbols in a linear fashion in the typewriter, which resulted in the development of the computer. The work of Kittler's middle period is entitled *Gramophone, Film, Typewriter* (1999).

These apparently total methods of recording, storage and transmission, in contrast to the subjective and partial accounts afforded by print, allowed new relations of presence and absence (to hear and see the voice and images of the dead, for example), and also introduced new possibilities of the manipulation of records, through various techniques of editing. At the same time as the possibility of complete record and recall appeared within one's grasp it became impossible to place trust in the records obtained, for the different processes of editing, of selection, cutting, re-recording, splicing and so forth, remain invisible to the hearer or viewer. These dilemmas – of persuasion, plausibility and trust – accompany every new medium; nonetheless, the effects of these new media may be judged extreme in terms of recasting diverse social relationships, including concepts relating to place and time, both because of their powers of recording potentially all details within a given range and because of the undetectable nature of editing in the final product. Furthermore, the technologies did not remain static, but developed in extraordinary ways, allowing the development of radio and then radar as the physics of soundwaves was explored, and the invention of the cinema and lasers in the progressive exploitation of the properties of higher wavelengths, together with the production of machines that could process information on the basis of the linear stream of symbols initially handled by the typewriter, with the development of digitalization, logic circuits and parallel processing.

Kittler also brought this broader perspective to a focus around the effects of the Second War, considered as an event marked by the acceleration of these branches of technological invention. I shall consider a single essay,[3] a review of Thomas Pynchon's novel *Gravity's Rainbow* (1973), taking from

---

3   'Media and drugs in Pynchon's Second World War' (1987), in Kittler (2013: 84–98).

it the framework of analysis he sketches, which serves to introduce certain features of the context in which flying saucers emerged.

Military technology and powers of communication

The interest of the piece is that Kittler focusses attention on the creative capacity of the military-technological constellation. His argument develops in two parts. As the first stage of his argument, he proposes that all the technologies of the present period were effectively invented in the context of weapons development during the Second World War and exploited commercially after the War. He points to magnetic tape, colour film, radar, VHF (Very High Frequency radio) and computers (Kittler 2013: 85), while the focus of the piece is the invention of rocket technology (V-2 rockets, the theme of Pynchon's novel). The relation of technology and the arms industry can of course be extended to cover an earlier period, but the relationship took on a new intensity in the Second War and remains important.

Kittler develops the argument that, behind the struggle between armies and nations, there was competition between technological industries, with the aim of first meeting the threat of rival developments, and then matching or imitating them, before finally surpassing them. New technologies were imitated and incorporated in an effort of overcoming. These dialectical processes involved the collection of technical information through intelligence, and anticipation of the potential of future developments;[4] this focus represents a shift away from a concern with diplomatic secrets, and even a lessening of interest in the movements of armies and equipment, towards the business of design and manufacture – a concern with blueprints, statistics, organizational plans and the like. And we may remark this frame, of intelligence sources and committees for appraisal of intelligence, reporting to higher authorities, was important in the development of flying saucer reports.

---

4   See Hinsley et al. (1980) and Jones (1978).

In this perspective, the War may be understood, rather than being a struggle between nations, as a series of exchanges between German and American technological industries, exchanges which accelerated during the War, exemplified in the developments of missile technology (the invention of liquid fuels and of techniques of detonation before impact), and which, after the War, took the form of transfers of technology, with the removal of men – knowledge – designs and techniques to the States. Competition may also be understood as a form of cooperation.

Kittler takes this aspect of his argument a step further: the War may be understood not primarily as a struggle between armies and nations, but rather as a competition for 'allocation and priority ... among different technologies, Plastics, Electronics, Aircraft' (Kittler 2013: 85, citing Pynchon). The story is not then even competition between different firms for business, but a struggle for priority between forms of technological life. Kittler's object is this technological world structure which came into being towards the end of the War and which continues to organize the post-War world, with effects to the present. Our concern is to locate flying saucers with respect to this totalizing structure ordering not only resource distribution but also interpretation and action.

The second part of Kittler's argument concerns the role of media, which offer a series of representations of the world that has been created, both exploiting and developing some of its features but, at the same time, in large part concealing the motive force of the struggles between forms of technological life.

As media work through technological means, the possibilities of the media developed in close relation to developments in military technology. In the first place, the media deal in information, in their essential tasks of recording, storage and dissemination, and so developments in information handling are common to both parties. The various media benefit from and are changed by the inventions made in the course of the development of military technologies. Techniques of recording, storage and transmission were revolutionized in the course of the War, whether to do with sound, film, or broadcasting, as was the business of manipulation and communication of information through these media. All post-War media and the range of tasks with which they were concerned – entertainment, information, advertising and so forth – bear the imprint of the War period.[5]

Kittler then makes a more controversial claim, for he regards specific media and details of their functioning as in some sense controlled by the underlying technological world structure and, in particular, as concealing 'the truth of the technological world' (the title of the collection of essays). On the one hand, any narrative or representation of the underlying struggles of different technologies would serve to conceal these more fundamental operations, because there is no 'story' to these competitions for resources. We might say that technical innovation takes place in a different space to that of representation. On the other hand, Kittler also proposes that these representations that conceal are among the products of technical operations; we are not simply dealing in military-technical production on the one side and media productions (the technical means of which are ever-enhanced) on the other, but in integrated, what he calls 'semiotechnical', operations whereby technical constellations produce fictive representations through the media. There is then a far tighter relation proposed between technical production and media representations than is commonly supposed, and we might begin to see how military business, including reports, might tie in with the production of newspapers, broadcasts, and films, as well as with the science fiction milieu. The histories we will investigate, of the Air Force's involvement in the early life of flying saucers, of the public nature of the space programme, and of the series of civilian sightings, all illustrate this tight relationship between production and representation.

Kittler points to two features of what we may call the imaginary space created by the media which transpose characteristics of the military-technical constellation. These features are what he terms manipulations of the time axis, which I would term 'time travelling', and paranoia. Both these features need further examination.

---

5   We might think of Packard's *The Hidden Persuaders* (1957) or, somewhat later, Tofler's *Future Shock* (1970). And the whole sequence of books on the changing nature of the American personality, from Riesman's *The Lonely Crowd* (1950) onwards, could be analysed in this perspective.

Time travelling

Following Pynchon, Kittler takes the instance of the V-2 rocket as emblematic of the first characteristic: the missile travels at faster than the speed of sound, so that the explosion occurs before the sound of the approach flight, apparently reversing the sequence of cause and effect. It is emblematic because the present period – defined by the 'semiotechnics' that have emerged in the acceleration of wartime technologies – is one in which 'the idea of cause and effect itself' is threatened.

In the account I want to offer, this breakdown of cause and effect may be attributed to the repeated failure of previously secure orders that allowed measurement: under these conditions, representations fail, and narratives not only of cause but also of time, identity, and knowledge become problematic. We shall return to the notion of the collapse of second order categories at the end of this section.

This loss of reliable causal structures may be traced in a number of features of the media. Kittler points first to the shift from narrative to information. In modern warfare, there is no possibility of making sense of experience, and the focus is instead on 'blueprints, statistics, and secret commands' (Kittler 2013: 87). Experience is fragmented, and permeated by mythical forms, while military attention is paid to documentary sources, to 'circuit diagrams, differential equations, business contracts and organizational charts' (Kittler 2013: 88). We might note in passing that the fragmentation of experience, the importance of documents, and the loss of any sense of time or temporal sequence are all standard tropes of modernist literature, from the First War on. And, returning to Kittler, because information is originally secret, concealed from the enemy and not shared among the population, it will only emerge slowly and be made sense of retrospectively; indeed, 'secret files ... become accessible to the extent that the goals they articulate have become reality – to the extent, that is, that they no longer need to be kept secret' (Kittler 2013: 88–89). Under these conditions, we might conclude, understanding has a temporal structure, and memory is never certain and always open to revision.

Kittler is concerned to point, second, to the importance of film in portraying a world in which narrative chains fail and in which memory can be manipulated or dissolved. Film began as a series of freeze-frame photographs, allowing motion to be broken down into component parts, and then the reproduction of motion by playing a succession of frames. In the simplest instance of manipulation, there is the possibility of reversing a sequence. With the development of cutting (shots taken from different angles) and montage (editing a sequence of cuts), there emerged further possibilities of exploring and manipulating time, so that cinema can show things that neither theatre nor life can show.

Kittler makes a number of related observations. The first (compare Virilio 1989) is that 'time-axis manipulations' are crucial to a form of warfare that depends on speed and information. Whether we are concerned with military, technological or propaganda operations, these cannot be effective without temporal abbreviations, extensions, and reversals. The medium of literature is unable to deal with these manipulations (at least, we may add, in popular form); in order to deal with physical time, technical media must be employed.

The second is that moving cameras were developed as an aspect of the development of weapons, to study in slow motion the flight first of bullets and then (using improved cameras) of missiles. The formal ground for this mutual development lies in film's being the technological medium which mimics the mathematical practice of integration. Kittler points to the parallel between the simple integration of successive frames in film, producing the illusion of continuous movement, and the use of the technique of integration – of the differential calculus – in, for example, resolving the problem of how to guide unmanned missiles to a target. Cameras had to be developed to study the dependent variables of time-axis manipulations in order to optimize weapons of destruction.

We might ask how fair is this account? Cinema was developed in co-operation with the needs of defence industries – essentially, the development of equipment to study the trajectories of projectiles. However, the film industry could then portray such varied effects of modern warfare as the explosion of a missile before it is heard – the emblematic reversal of cause and effect – and, by a simple montage playing with time order, portray such features of warfare as the anticipated reduction of cities to ruins, and the emergence of future conditions out of ruins (as in the construction of German factories, their ruin through bombing, and the transfer of their processes to new sites in the States, together with post-War reconstruction). Film can show us the simultaneity that appears to triumph over time, chance, and place, with all its conditions present at once. Moreover, cinema plays a direct role in the war effort by fabricating simple narratives in news reels and films of entertainment, both with their simplified story arc and the things left unsaid.

Kittler is concerned, however, to indicate the role of cinema in creating the formal time conditions lived within the modern 'semiotechnical' world structure. In such a structure, dominated by technologies of information and information transfers, memory with its chains of cause and effect is dissolved, and experience consists in events, created from one moment to the next. Under these conditions, time sequences can be manipulated, so that later forms may appear to be designed into the development of projects (American space shots began as German weapons; industries are created and destroyed in one place, for their technological innovations to be exploited commercially elsewhere); and origins may be falsified retrospectively. Moreover, things such as manned space flight (and UFOs) may be anticipated by film or fiction and, indeed, reversals of cause and effect can go further, so that the creation of fictitious histories can give rise to realizations: interpretations, jokes, even lies, can turn out to alter the past giving rise to novel effects[6] (for these claims, see Kittler 2013: 92). This is the puzzle of fictions which in due course may 'come true', in acts that look like clairvoyance.

So, in a world where the collapse of second order categories is prevalent or repeated, temporal sequences of cause and effect become unreliable, and this condition can be mapped by metaphysical representations in some respects so that correspondences emerge, and it appears, without any present experienced unity, that some kind of mind is behind the phenomena, revelations, elections and so forth. While I tend to look for collapse and remapping to explain these forms, Kittler looks to the mindless competition of technological forms played out in military-industrial capitalism.

6   cf. Borges' story 'Tlön, Uqbar, Orbis Tertius' (Borges 1970).

In sum, film, as the physical medium which allows the manipulation of time and so the reversal of cause and effect, is implicated in the development of weapons technology; it also serves to conceal that technological complex; and it leaks into 'real life', producing attitudes, memories, roles and phenomena which gain autonomous existence. These leakages occur in the detail of personal, mental and sexual lives, including brushes with death and, as we shall see, with interplanetary beings.

A final comment on this topic: as already noted, there are a number of motifs present which surface in modernist literature, and which relate to the manufactured nature of experience when living in a technologically influenced world. Romanticism – portraying a relation to nature – becomes impossible, as does realism – based simply in human social relations or a commitment to a scientific worldview. Instead, personality becomes multiple, one can move to and fro in time, and narrative breaks down into short episodes without an overall plot, but which nevertheless gestures towards some kind of mysterious key. In this perspective, the appearance of flying saucers is an aspect of modernism – part of the run of modernist ideas between roughly 1910 and 1975. And that leaves us with the question of what then happens when modernism begins to falter? This gives some context to the shift in the literature concerned with flying saucer sightings to alien abductions and recovered memory from the 1960s onward, together with the move to mental explanations more generally. We may remark that we are not dealing in technological determinism of any kind, but in mutations in world structures.

Paranoia as a social condition

With this account in mind of the complex and generative structure of semiotechnical space, centring on manipulations around the time axis, we can begin to appreciate the force of Kittler's last feature, the 'truth' of paranoia. Once again, this feature has a number of aspects to be considered.

If the world lacks any overall narrative (despite ideological clashes of friend and foe), but instead is a matter of 'blueprints, statistics, and secret commands', each actor has to seek to decipher signs concerning the activities of the underlying competing technologies in order to understand what he or she is confronted with. In essence, if information composes the vital matters of living, intelligence techniques have to be adopted in order to live. We might suggest that this is perhaps why stories of detection are a feature of this period, where the hero or antihero deciphers the significance of signs in the world to uncover what is going on. Again, there are hints available in popular culture: we could place the contrast between Holmes' assumption of being able to read a coherent world and that of post-War chaos at the borders of modernism in the 1920s. The 1940s were marked by 'Film Noir', with solitary figures deciphering a bad world. By the 1980s, the noir detective was a figure of the past, used only as a self-conscious reference or trope.

If deciphering is the key method, one technique is to construe patterns of events and to seek correlations between apparently independent probabilistic distributions for, in such seeming coincidences, the perspective of a protagonist emerges. Through the correlation of statistical patterns, a potential plot may be discerned in a subjectless world. The correlation of patterns necessarily introduces a 'metaphysical' perspective, for, in seeking a rationale for the coincidence of two series of events – a coincidence which is no coincidence but significant – one introduces the prospect of a hidden, mind-like, third entity which explains these synchronicities. There are plenty of candidates for this third entity: the intelligence and the security services, the military, developers of new technologies and industrial contractors, politicians and businessmen, marketers and advertisers, the people in the media. Or any combination of parties, in a spectrum of overlapping interests. There is after all plenty of evidence of cooperation, of concealment of facts, and of manipulations of categories, persons and events. Flying saucers and their alien occupants can be readily fitted into this kaleidoscope.

For this reason, Kittler, having looked at the change in narrative technique demanded by modern warfare, and the implication of the new subject – the constellation of technologies – in the experience of everyday life, turns to the topic of paranoia; paranoia is perhaps Kittler's central concern, his study of *Geist* in its modern, technical form ('the truth of the technological world'), which the two preliminaries – a semiotechnical world and manipulations of the time-axis – serve to set up and make comprehensible.

Paranoia is related to agency in this account: it is the nature of the world that is being created by the semiotechnologies, which manufacture extraordinary correspondences, and so, at the same time, the reasonable key to the individual's experience of this world. In the first place, the world is in part constructed by non-obvious processes – competition between technological forms of life, the effective cooperation of enemies through transfers of information, the focus on information rather than narrative. Nothing is as it seems; just as seeming enemies may turn out to be allies, so allies may turn out to be enemy spies.

In the second place, the task of any actor is to collect and decipher information, sometimes on behalf of other agencies, in order to place it in some never-completed narrative. As remarked, this is the period of the investigator, gradually revealing plots which link together disparate parts of society. Films are made up of flashbacks and double crosses revealed after the event, together with a certain vision of commercial interest, sexual attraction and death as the constructed and constructing forces of life's possibilities, forces which are always glimpsed but never fully apprehended.

In the third place, the representations produced by various cultural milieus, whether in literature or film, play with the forms used by the new technologies – time reversals, suspicion, the deciphering of connections – but at the same time conceal the reason behind or mainspring for these representations. The technical complex acts as a mind – or has mind-like properties – but can only be discerned in its effects, and can only be charted retrospectively, when dossiers and sources can be opened, and the issues are no longer live. The social sciences of the period, particularly psychology (behaviourism), are shaped by the semiotechnical structures but not revealing of their mechanisms. The productive forces control the forms of representation and effect their own concealment. In this regard, Kittler has a strongly Marxist flavour.

Paranoia is clinically defined as confusing words with things, but under these conditions, paranoia may be a means of understanding. This attitude contains truth because the actor has to search for clues, for coincidences that turn out to be correspondences, and to draw out the significance of linking certain patterns. But it also alerts the actor to those apparent reversals of time, where fictions give rise to reality, effects precede their cause, and ends are anticipated in processes. Moreover, because productive forces control processes of revelation, there may have been retrospective editing of sources (which we may call the 'Soviet Encyclopedia' phenomenon) so that records – and memories – become unreliable (which may be related to the rise of 'recovered memory' in the later part of the period). And, finally, even the desire of the searcher after truth may have been subject to construction.

Because understanding, memory and desire may all be mutable, the actors can have no straightforward continuity of identity but instead may undergo exchange – swapping positions – and metamorphoses. Kittler, drawing on Pynchon, suggests that drugs imitate the effects of this world condition, allowing perception of the transformation of the same person in different roles and the 'identity' of distinct conditions. Drugs therefore mimic the 'recovery of lost memory' (as does hypnosis) and the anticipation of future states, but, he adds in pessimistic mode, both past and future are told in banal plot lines, as if the actors lived in a soap opera world.

And we may add, these hallucinatory exchanges and transformations may be observed in the productions of science fiction writers and the military, as the one detects plots and the other chases unidentified objects. Nobody is left as they were, and writing (reporting) is caught up in the processes of the subject matter, the semiotechnical complex.

Is it possible to escape these toils and to write a clear account of the processes at work? Kittler's solution is to oppose the state of paranoia – 'the foreboding reading of a single coherent scheme that can be manipulated' – to what he calls an attitude of 'anti-paranoia' – 'where nothing connects to anything'. And so he sets the traditional narrative, where the hero reduces the ramifying chains of possibility until a structure or solution is reached, against the anti-paranoid position, in which the opposite happens – information multiplies and hence entropy increases, with no order being imposed. This position appears to be perilously close to post-modernism, which Kittler, however, despises.

It is nevertheless a clear position, if one accepts the totalizing power of the semiotechnical structure to recast the past as well as the present and the future. Yet I suspect this is an exaggerated fear: all anthropology and history demand 'dead stretches' or archives in order to make sense, and the problem is to restore a sense of life and its processes to these records, discerning the questions to which these documents represent answers within a precise context and time. Because the records are the product of processes and, precisely, not a record of them, one has to have recourse to various forms of supplementation, importing models, making comparisons, correcting readings. Without creating a single narrative, which seems to be the secret of paranoia, it is possible to interrogate materials and to make sense of them, including making sense of moments of collapse in orders of measurement and the multiple registrations of such occasions as events, and to trace this history.

Commentary

What can we take from Kittler for our purposes? The major themes appear to be the non-representability of alterations in second order categories (changes in technical possibility), which are expressed in reversals of time – so that fictions become true – and the truth of paranoia – take your fears for reality, suspect conspiracies and so forth. Underlying this account, there is the notion that the semiotechnical structure alters perceptions and matches them to its needs for secrecy and information, so that the truth of the advanced scientific world – because of its military and industrial organization – is metaphysical: there is a world mind to explain the significance of apparent coincidences. Can't we have the first elements – category collapse, time travelling, and even the imputation of purpose – without joining in the paranoid narrative? Nevertheless, there is a good deal of interest in this account.

These broad conditions persisted in the post-War period: the technologies invented in the War continued to compete for resources, with a variety of narratives conveyed through the media concealing much of the point of these struggles. Likewise, there was exchange of technologies between nations, organizations and companies, and exchanges too between technologies. Flying saucers clearly relate to rockets and the development of space travel, as well as expansions in the size of the known universe. Computers and radar played their part.

But they also owe a good deal to the developments of the various media. As well as having exceptional acceleration (flying faster than the fastest current aircraft), flying saucers behave like objects on film: they can hover, accelerate and change direction without physical constraint. They can appear in this way to respond directly to the intentions of their pilots, so that they express thought without mediation. In this, they resemble radio, too, which offers direct communication without bodily presence: the voice heard makes no reference to the physical infrastructure which permits it. And communications from flying saucers arrive in a comparable fashion, telepathically – bypassing problems of acoustics and translation – and conveying moral messages of peace and fraternity. News of these new phenomena are spread through the press and radio by press agencies, by telegraph and telephone and teleprinter. Flying saucers were constructed in part by new techniques of recording and transmission. These are the kinds of elements at work in the history we have to consider. And, as we shall see, paranoia as a social condition has its place there as well.

Kittler's analysis describes practically every feature of the world in which flying saucers appear, one marked by extraordinary and continuous technological innovation, militarized to a high degree, in which government agencies concerned themselves with the control of aspects of the public mind, and within which common experience was created without reference to the underlying means of its production. In this world, previously secure means of measurement, categories by which we located and made sense of new things, broke down repeatedly, so that new styles of definition had to be invented alongside the appearance of these novelties. Appearances, then, were detached from knowable conditions; reliable connections were hard or impossible to discern; and objects of the kind discussed in the first chapter, where real and imaginary elements coexisted and continually exchanged place, could materialize and make their unpredictable effects felt.

II. From the point of view of experience

If Kittler focusses on changes at the large-scale, he also gives hints about alterations in the individual's experience of this new world, which is in large part made up of 'leakages' from the technological complex into ordinary lives, found in the intimate details of attitudes, memories, roles and the phenomena encountered. In this new condition, sense can only be made of individual lives in retrospect, and the organizing forces glimpsed by these backwards acts of insight. This perspective is explored in detail in a novel from the same period, of which I now offer a summary – the first of several works of fiction to serve the argument. The reader should bear in mind possible parallels with encounters with aliens, noticing that, even at this early date, we are dealing with an expansion in the nature of possible experience.

'The Island of Doctor Morel'

The story – Bioy Casares' novel *The Invention of Morel* – was published in Argentina in 1940.[7] It is an exemplary fictional account of the effects of media technology. It provides an instructive parallel in this regard with better-known examples of North American science fiction.

The narrator is a political exile and former prisoner, on the run from the oppressive powers that govern his Southern American country. We are not told his crime. He finds a boat and flees to an unpopulated island in the Pacific, which has been indicated to him as a possible refuge, although he has also been warned that visitors are afflicted by a wasting disease. There he finds a deserted residence on high ground, with a swimming pool nearby, and, set in the tidal swamp below, a mill which generates electricity for the building by harnessing the force of the tides.

---

7   The story has been filmed for television; see Claude-Jean Bonnardot's 1967 adaptation, *L'invention de Morel*, ina éditions, series 'les inédits fantastiques' (2012).

At first, he occupies the decayed building and describes its condition. It could be a hotel or sanitorium; it includes a series of rooms on the ground floor, a main staircase and a servants' spiral stair, and a number of bedroom suites upstairs, together with a basement with rooms filled with mysterious machines. The swimming pool is well made and has been taken over by snakes, frogs, and aquatic insects. But after a few days, he is forced to abandon the house and retreat to the swamp because he is disturbed by the arrival of intruders: 'suddenly, unaccountably, on this oppressive summerlike night, the grassy hillside has become crowded with people who dance, stroll up and down, and swim in the pool, as if this were a summer resort like Los Teques or Marienbad' (Bioy Casares 2003: 10–11).

The arrival of the visitors changes the situation: he begins to keep a diary – the narrative we have – and has to conceal himself to prevent his detention and arrest; he therefore has to hide himself in the swamp where he is continually threatened by the irregular tides, the unhealthy conditions, and the inedible plants. It also introduces a new element, for he is attracted by one of the party, a woman who, each day, goes and sits on the rocks to watch the sunset, where he waits, hidden, to observe her. Other actors appear in the narrative; one day, he resents people fishing from the rocks and those watching them, for they prevent him from coming closer to the woman; another day, he feels annoyance and the stirrings of jealousy on seeing her conversing with a bearded tennis player. After a few days, he confronts her directly, but she ignores him, as if he were invisible. This treatment is repeated on other occasions. Still hidden, he tracks her developing relationship with the tennis player – we learn he is called Morel, she Faustine – until, believing he has been seen by another visitor, he retreats for several days to the swamp.

When he returns, he witnesses further conversation between Morel and Faustine; they meet in the same place, repeat the same gestures and words, and yet it seems to the narrator their relationship has moved on; that in the meantime, perhaps, there has been a brief intimacy, but she at least now regrets it and has withdrawn. Moved by his dislike of Morel, the narrator approaches and insults him; Morel walks towards him so that he has to move out of the way, yet both the visitors continue to act as if he were not there. Humiliated and alone, the narrator walks up the hill, determined to give himself up, but he finds the hill deserted. He searches the house; everything is as it was before the visitors' arrival, twenty days before. There is no evidence of any visitors; nothing has been moved, and the untidy and neglected state of things has been restored.

We have met enough anomalies to raise questions: the visitors' complete indifference to the narrator's presence, the exact repetition of forms of words and gestures, and, finally, the restoration of the environment and conditions to those he had experienced on arriving on the island. The narrator copes with the first by speculating about motives, the second by reflecting on the real reasons we have for speaking and writing. But to explain the third, he has to wonder both at the facts and the powers of memory, and to ask whether he has been in a delirium induced by drugs contained in the roots he has been forced to eat. Or, whether, as an alternative explanation, his persecutors – the system of justice he had fled from – have the power to alter mind and recollection.

A second act ensues. The narrator searches through the abandoned property. He finds the lights do not work and the machines in the basement are silent, and attributes this to the recent low tides. Yet, during his search, he hears the machinery start up and the lights come on, and, simultaneously, a second visit appears to be in mid-course. The scene has changed from abandoned ruin to elaborate social life in a few minutes. The narrator finds the same party as before, eating in the dining room.

He continues to watch as the party breaks up. When he tries to leave, he finds he cannot open a door, nor any of the windows. In the morning, he finds some doors open, others immovable. He threads his way through the people talking in the assembly hall and jumps through the open first-floor window to the ground below. He returns to the ravine and there is no pursuit.

This second appearance of the visitors is also accompanied by a strange meteorological phenomenon, for the following day there were two suns and, the night, two moons. It was some kind of mirage, accompanied by intense heat. From his position in the swamp, the narrator can see the visitors come and go on the hillside and ponders his relationship to them. He may have the illness associated with the island and be imagining them. Or the polluted air of the marshes and his diet may have made him invisible, though, against this, the insects, animals and birds know he is there. He has more or less discarded the notion that the visitors' indifference to him is feigned, part of a police plot to capture him. Another possibility, they could be from another planet and use their faculties for different ends and so not register him. Likewise, their alien language may have different meanings, although they appear to speak French. Again, he could be in an asylum of which Morel is the director. Or he could be dead and the others spirits 'at a different phase of … metamorphosis' (Bioy Casares 2003: 52), and they could be moving in separate, incommunicable worlds.

As he watches the sea under the heat of the two suns, a large white freighter appears close to the island; a launch is lowered and a man in a uniform disembarks and walks up the hill. Faustine and a group of friends walk down to the pool, which the narrator believes to be filled with leaves, dead birds and live snakes and frogs; Faustine dives in and the others join her. Afterwards, they head back to the house.

This second series of anomalies is more striking than the first: the sudden reversal of conditions, the resumption of a story in mid-telling, the continued ignoring of the intruder's presence, the two suns in the sky, the sudden appearance of the boat. It is as if the narrator were in the midst of a film being projected, a record of life taking place elsewhere, and this is the state of affairs about to be revealed.

Morel's explanation

The narrator overhears Morel invite one guest to a meeting later that evening. Morel also invites Faustine, interrupting the narrator who is declaring his love to her out loud; again, he is apparently invisible to them both. The evening passes, with music from a gramophone and dancing. Around midnight, the narrator enters the house and watches through a half-open door as Morel and the others arrange the room for a lecture. Once the guests have assembled, Morel begins to address them, reading from a script which the narrator collects at the conclusion to the evening, so the talk is transcribed accurately for the reader.

The gist of Morel's talk is that he has recorded the guests without their permission. More than simply filming them and recording their voices, he has used his latest invention: all their actions have been recorded, complete in every detail and for the entire seven days, and this record will live forever. He had not told them at the outset, for knowledge would have spoiled their spontaneity; as a consequence of this ignorance, they have had a pleasant week together, but this week is not a transient moment: instead, 'I have given you a pleasant eternity' (Bioy Casares 2003: 66).

So far, technology has allowed communication at a distance for the senses of sight and sound, employing the appropriate 'vibrations' in 'television, motion pictures, photography' for the first and 'radio, the phonograph, the telephone' for the second (Bioy Casares 2003: 68). Morel's work has been to 'apply this principle to the other senses, to all the other senses'. He has built on the work of others and cooperated with some established firms, searching for 'waves and vibrations that had previously been unattainable' and devising 'instruments to receive and transmit them' (Bioy Casares 2003: 69). In this fashion, as well as perfecting phonograph records and photographic images, he has worked on the olfactory, thermal, and tactile sensations. When played together, these recordings allow one to reproduce people and situations in their entirety, so that 'an observer will not realize that they are images' (Bioy Casares 2003: 70). The projections were to resemble those of motion pictures or television, Morel continues; his original belief was that the reproductions would be images but not the real thing, for 'images of persons would lack consciousness of themselves (like the characters in a motion picture)'. However, he came to revise this point of view, for 'when all the senses are synchronized, the soul emerges ... When ... [a person] existed for the senses of sight, hearing, taste, smell, and touch, ... [that person] herself was actually there' (Bioy Casares 2003: 71).

The narrator's reluctant conclusion is that the visitors are 'illusions ... a new kind of photograph' (Bioy Casares 2003: 74), and that he is alone 'on an island inhabited by artificial ghosts ... in love with one of those images' (Bioy Casares 2003: 75).

Implications

The principal focus of the story is a meditation on the nature of desire, revealed by these conditions: rethinking the relation between the imagination and memory in the repetitions of a love affair. As the narrator reflects, 'perhaps we always want the person we love to have the existence of a ghost' (Bioy Casares 2003: 75). From our perspective, however, the interest lies in the imaginative space created by the mechanisms of total recording. We may think that the presence of the loved one may be to the viewer alone, not self-presence to the image; this limit appears to be a by-product of the motivation through desire. Love (in this account) projects its desire onto the loved one as if she were a screen; her own reactions and desires are not in any respect considered, and indeed, constitute an inscrutable residue that constantly creates problems for the lover. But the narrator comes to address this problem.

The meaning of Morel's project is now quite clear: the week of the house party, with its life of thoughts and feelings, has been captured by the machinery and will be repeated endlessly. And although one says repeated, each moment will be new because each actor will have only the memories he or she possesses in the original moment of recording, and so 'the future, left behind many times, will maintain its attributes forever' (Bioy Casares 2003: 76).

The notion of a total record being replayed continually, interrupted only when the tides are too low to provide power, explains many of the anomalies we have encountered. The presence and absence of images, the sudden reversals between the week of the house party and the present of the ruin, the doubling up of celestial bodies when the seasons recorded and in reality do not match, the indifference of actors in one time to those in another, are all explained. And there is a certain poignancy to the way the narrator reads meanings that are not there into the actions of the images, imagining they might share common schemes of interpretation and seeking reasons that relate to himself to explain their actions. The careful scrutiny to which he subjects Faustine's character and motives becomes ridiculous when considered in light of the new evidence and contains a warning concerning our everyday practices. She is not indifferent to him, nor inclined to favour him, nor choosing between two lovers; he does not exist for her. At the same time, these observations allow us to see the importance of repetition in everyday life: each apparent repetition, however exact, may carry a different significance, allow new interpretation, join to other elements and situations in the past, and create new possibilities in the future.

Beyond these lessons, there are further complications to consider, for at certain points these two worlds can bleed into one another, causing a further set of anomalous incidents when each effects alteration in the other. These are the business of the last part of the story.

The narrator begins by reflecting that, given these means of total recording, in principle 'nothing is lost', and that the vibrations left behind by any event may one day be isolated and realized, so that 'it will be possible for all souls, both those that are intact, and the ones whose elements have been dispersed, to have immortality' (Bioy Casares 2003: 78).

He starts to live deliberately in parallel with the recorded episode. He moves back into the house (which we now understand to be a museum, a collection of images), safe from the tides and the swamp. With the images present, he understands why some doors are impossible to open: if closed when filmed, they remain that way when projected. He gradually explores the details of the week, finding no signs of any intimate relationship between Morel and Faustine, though doubt never entirely leaves him. Further, he speculates whether the recorded images feel and think, and even whether they may then employ this repertoire of thoughts and experience in new combinations ('transpositions' – Bioy Casares 2003: 82). In which case, we might add, it becomes increasingly difficult to separate out copies from the originals. The narrator argues that the images will not encounter new objects, but they will understand things in time and space just as we do, and the conditions of our life may obtain in this form of survival. He adds, 'a rotating eternity may seem atrocious to an observer, but it is quite acceptable to those who dwell there' (Bioy Casares 2003: 85).

This repeated life, he sees, has its advantages. 'Free from bad news and disease, they live forever as if each thing were happening for the first time; they have no memory of anything that happened before. And the interruptions caused by the rhythm of the tides keep the repetition from being implacable' (Bioy Casares 2003: 85). In comparison, his own life appears 'irreparably haphazard', in which past acts can neither be repaired nor redeemed.

Beyond living in parallel with the life of the images and speculating whether one can in fact claim any superiority for this 'real' life in comparison with the life of simulacra, the narrator also takes a practical interest in the machinery, his first object being to see whether he can control its working by other means than reliance on the tides, in this way sustaining Faustine's presence. This investigation leads to the final step, as the two worlds become ever more engaged.

As he explores the house, he begins to find indications of his previous interventions, evidence that it is possible to alter conditions within the record. This is presumably because the business of recording is also taking place within the cycle of exact repetition. As he explores the machinery, he finds some equipment for 'receiving' (filming), recording and projecting images. He makes some experiments, filming 'flowers, leaves, flies, frogs' (Bioy Casares 2003: 92) and seeing them reproduced exactly as three-dimensional images. He also imprudently films his left hand. The original objects, which he calls 'transmitters', die: the leaves and flowers after five or six hours; the frogs after fifteen; the flies appear to do better. But 'the copies survive; they are incorruptible' (Bioy Casares 2003: 93). He speculates as to why the specimens have died, but then realizes that his left hand is beginning to burn and the skin to fall off.

Here, then, we have an exchange between the two spheres, between images and real life. It leads the narrator to reread Morel's text, noting that he hints at the deaths of those experimented upon. This decay presumably explains the wasting disease associated with the island. The narrator also recalls that 'some people are afraid of having their images reproduced because they believe that their souls will be transferred to the images and will die' (Bioy Casares 2003: 94). The possibility is that the 'transmitters' – the living objects – lose their souls when 'photographed by the machines'. In which case, it is possible that the images have the souls of the originals (and so that the image of Faustine may 'be' Faustine).

The narrator's last actions are to insert himself into the record of the week. First, he studies the week exactly and in detail, rehearsing every action, thinking up replies to remarks, participating in the conversation.

Then, he turns on the 'receivers of simultaneous action', so that he is recorded in this integrated, choreographed behaviour. Finally, he arranges the records so that the new version is played in each future repetition. He succeeds in overcoming any self-consciousness so that, 'if my image has the same thoughts I had when it was taken ... then I shall spend eternity in the joyous contemplation of Faustine' (Bioy Casares 2003: 101).

As the price for this recording, his body begins to disintegrate; he can follow the process in a screen of mirrors. And he leaves the pious hope that some future technology will be invented which can 'assemble disjointed presences' (Bioy Casares 2003: 103) and that he will be allowed to enter Faustine's consciousness.

III. Repetition and truth

We are dealing with images produced by technical means, and so have never left Kittler's view of the world. The narrator makes reference to Swedenborg's heavens and we end in the same place, dealing in encounters with other worlds, with spirits and aliens, and with non-human minds and the paradoxes of time that accompany their appearances. For, although the point of the invention appears to be the linear reproduction of a specific stretch of time – a realist account, then, with all feelings and experiences intact – the *repetition* of this literal world with all the truths of its actions to be discovered (Did their feet touch beneath the table? What went on behind that door on that occasion?) moves us to a world of multiple, incompatible pasts and the possibility of making new connections and of forming new relations which will alter both the future and the past. We have moved from action to observation, from intervention to deciphering.

This is the power of technologies of recording, storing, and reproducing images. Images become autonomous, so that we cannot tell them apart from 'real life', and have effects within that real life. We therefore impute mind and intention to them. Reciprocally, 'real life' figures take on the properties of images: they become characters in narratives in which truth and fiction are mixed.

Technology and its accompanying media therefore assist in producing a state of affairs in which certain rules operate, new rules which are a feature of the contemporary world. One of those features is a certain 'cinematic' quality to much of life, seen in the kind of plots we expect to find at work and our treatment both of ourselves and others within these narratives. In a word, we believe *experience* to be a primary feature of the world, and experience has a repertoire of characteristic plots. We run through this repertoire in an endless cycle of repetitions, working with a company of stereotypic figures and accompanied by a familiar soundtrack. For us as moderns, it is an everyday matter to revisit lost time; it is not even a cause for reflection.

Lessons learnt

What have we learned from Bioy Casares' story? In sum, we now know we live in a world of images, one where we have become images, or taken on certain of their properties. Both the worlds of realism and imagination are made relative once it is seen they are the product of images, created by a process that populates the world with beings that can be read in either optic, as active subjects or as the passive objects of narratives. This is a state where persons and events take on qualities because of their interaction with other entities. In this instance, the narrator encounters the images of the house party and moves through a sequence of possible relations as he interacts with them and learns how to participate in their lives.

Initially, he projects his thoughts onto the images, interpreting their actions and imputing motives to them, for he presumes they have intentions towards him and tries to discern these impulses. Are they pretending not to have seen him? To what end – to lull his fears, to permit his arrest? And, with more intensity, are they using his relationship to Faustine for their own purposes? And what are her feelings towards him? How can we interpret her behaviour? It is possible to misread the actions of the house party in numerous ways, and these possibilities are accompanied by the narrator's vivid interior life (who, as a writer, is perhaps already given to these self-inflicted errors). He seeks to evaluate Faustine's behaviour as responding to him and to others and to detect changes in her attitude, in this fashion imagining new possibilities and knowing new disappointments. All these interpretations are the product of the encounter in a realistic idiom with ghosts (or aliens), images living their independent lives.

A second series of possibilities arise from trying to account for those anomalies already encountered: the narrator has to seek explanations for this vivid life taking place before him and in his mind. Are these hallucinations, produced by fever, exhaustion, or drugs absorbed from eating roots? Have his enemies – functionaries of the state in various capacities – the ability to manipulate his mind and present it with a sequence of deceptive experiences? Is he dead and viewing a spirit world which he cannot yet take part in? Or are these alien life forms, apparently mimicking human form and behaviour, but with nothing in common with human existence? These, we might say, are formal solutions, assuming an objective life form in parallel with his own but all adding notions of mental control, the power to act at a distance and to work by clairvoyance and telepathy. Projection onto images necessarily invokes notions of mind and mental powers, errors and fictions.

Then, a third set of possibilities arise from the realization that this parallel world is the product of a new technology, and the anomalies emerge because this parallel world flows into this life and, moreover, that it is vulnerable to human intervention, a flow in the opposite direction. So, on the one hand, we have the directly 'filmic' moments when the recording begins to play again or a fragment repeats, gaining new significance; there are moments of dislocation between the record and the meteorological seasons, resulting in two moons or irregular tides; there are the alternations between present decay and recorded elegance, in the condition of the swimming pool, and the fixity or mobility of doors and windows. In all these cases, the records impinge on the senses; they alter conditions in the present and, by so doing, multiply possible pasts and potential futures. In response to these effects, on the other hand, the narrator can undertake to insert himself into the past by present action – a form parallel to that of recovered memory – and can hope that, in some future state, juxtaposed images – which already possess certain autonomous powers of initiative – may achieve a mutual presence.

In this fashion, we grant life to images, and we come to wonder whether, in the present, we are more than images ourselves; whether, in short, life can be opposed to image, or whether everything shares elements of both original and copy. We live in a world where images give life to the living and vice versa, and where ghosts and their compeers serve as actors, joining groups, times, and places, while offering new possibilities and new resources for repair and renewal. We can claim that flying saucer reports illustrate this process to perfection.

For, as modern people, we live in the world as if it were composed of such images, although lacking the complex self-conscious apprenticeship the narrator underwent. The force of images lies in the affections they evoke in us, the unquestioned sense of reality and value we experience. Yet, given the infinite variety of possible interpretations, why do we settle for one of a small range of rival claims – is it a person or is it a recording, for example? The answer is collective habit – in this case, we meet plenty of people, we watch films, listen to the radio and so forth. The range of possible interpretation is given, although it evolves discontinuously over time, and we mobilize some part of it, appropriate to our education, small group, and life experience. In short, we each frame significant objects within a specific sense of memory, exploring the resources of collective narratives of past events shaping shared identities, which to a great extent determine what we see and feel and how we evaluate and react to each stimulus. One person might see an old statue, feeling little curiosity or interest in it, while another sees quite another object, a symbol of the exercise of cruel power in the past and indifference on the part of society to the consequences of that exercise in the present. It is no different with sightings: some part of the real world may pass without remark or significance or, on the contrary, be seen as a machine guided by intentions that are inscrutable, a condensation of effects of the technical and mediatic contemporary world. We may see reflected lights or we may see a space craft; the repertoire is set by the new conditions of recording, storage and transmission, and the experience of its different facets is real – felt and experienced by each one present and open too to interpretation by everyone who hears the report. Every image is made up by a mix of real and imaginary characteristics, a range formed by habit into certain familiar options. But the experience is in every case real, felt, and therefore certain, even if open to revision. That is the lesson of Bioy Casares' tale.

Yet this is not a position without its problems; images carry within them a series of limitations. In them, information comes to substitute for bodily life, including cooperation and conversation. In the tale of Morel's invention, we meet the accelerated decay of the body of any living thing that is recorded, as well as the disappearance of any pretence of initiative on the part of the images (even if they detect no difference in their sense of freedom and initiative in each repetition). The only possibility of initiative comes from without, in the actions of the narrator, for example. Nor could one be confident of the uses that machinery would be put to under any political regime. Paradoxically, despite the death of the body, desire or love appears to remain the best guarantee we have of deciphering the truth that is being hidden from us by the manipulation of appearances.

The appeal to images cannot then replace the spectrum of positions it allows; we need both action and observation, realism and imagination. This is as far as we can get: there are a series of tensions without resolution, effects and possibilities created by a civilization based on the possibility of total reproduction and therefore a social order containing both literal truth and the most complete deception, a civilization with machinery at its heart that generates new forms of difference and the passing of time. We now need to explore an instance of how a lasting content was given to this imaginative space.

CHAPTER 3

The Report on Unidentified Flying Objects

If certain modern forms of the imagination arise because of the close links between innovations in military technology and modern media, and these forms can on occasion be provided with a content – or co-opted – by the engagement of fictions with early products of this technical-mediatic world, the next problem is to track the realization of these imaginative hybrids in the contemporary world.

This chapter offers a study of the American Air Force's contribution to the flying saucer problem, approached through reading Edward Ruppelt's *The Report on Unidentified Flying Objects*, published in 1956. Ruppelt's *Report* is the only contemporary account from the early period of UFO sightings that gives an insider's view from the military perspective. In principle, it will allow us to escape from any anachronistic imposition of later views and to trace the emergence of an 'image' in its various stages. By image I mean both an object of thought – something perceived – and the framework that permits its apprehension. Both developed contingently; there was no preconceived or predetermined path of development. Rather, both incidents and the models that simultaneously allowed and made sense of these sightings each followed their own course, bowing to constraints and seizing their opportunities, and have to be reconstructed after the event. We are, then, dealing with a case study of a mobile object.

It is worth repeating that this chapter represents an investigation of a single book; it is not an objective account of the early history of the engagement of intelligence sources with flying saucers (were such an account possible), but a reconstruction of the writing of an important text and of its reception, use and revision by later scholars. It is a case study of the making and remaking of the image in question, which has been and continues to be highly influential; it sets many of the presuppositions still in play in analysing reports of UAPs (Unidentified Anomalous Phenomena), for example, and is worth considering in detail to trace the creation of this framework.

I. Ruppelt's contribution

Ruppelt was more than a witness to this episode of history; because of his systematic gathering and ordering of reports and his repeated efforts to investigate and gain evidence by scientific means, he was a major actor, responsible in part for recasting categories and the emergence of a new kind of object. It could be suggested that, without Ruppelt, 'Unidentified Flying Objects' would not have taken the form they did and would not have gained public credibility and, indeed, they might never have achieved the degree of reality they attained, at the time and subsequently. He was an important player in the appearance of UFOs and the understanding gained of them, and this was because of his public commitment to the scientific investigation of sightings and reports by the Air Force. There were traces of such a commitment before his time, but the subject was never pursued by the military with any thoroughness after his retirement, at least in the public's mind.[1] Because of that commitment, a good deal followed in terms of the history we are tracing.

Given his double role, both as someone recounting the story he was involved in as an actor, but also as a person who helped develop the categories in which that story is understood, the history we are concerned with has to be viewed recursively, and subsequent research comes to play an important part in the investigation. This research concerns classified documents from the period which have been made available because the information they contain can no longer be thought of as a security matter, and the process of Ruppelt's recasting of ideas and judgements can be tracked

---

[1] We will touch on aspects of a 'secret history', but these fall into another kind of history, that of the 'covert sphere' – for which term, see Melley (2012).

and reappraised on the basis of this new material. There is an on-going task of revision; just as Ruppelt was involved in decisions and judgements which altered relationships and understandings and affected later perspectives, so these relationships and ideas themselves are re-examined and re-evaluated by the later discoveries, recalling and adjusting the perspectives that had been developed. Swords and Powell (2012) offer a synthesis based on these newly released documents and provide supplementary materials allowing this recurrent history to be charted to an extent, so we can map the effects that emerge from Ruppelt's early commitment to research and the complex timeframe in which the sequence as a whole develops, a sequence where the future is real in the sense that it is a function neither of an origin nor of any determined end point. In other words, it is not uncovering a pre-existing object, but the appearance of something new.

A focus on novelty and emergence

What kind of thing are we looking at? In reading Ruppelt's account, we are concerned – as we have suggested – simultaneously with his objects of interest and with the frame within which they are made sense of. Or rather, to be more precise, we focus on the *emergence* of these objects and *shifts* in how their appearances are grasped. We are then interested in noting wider developments, some alteration associated with the introduction of a new technology, for example, or the impact of an incident with unexpected features, changes often signalled by a shift in vocabulary.

In developing this focus, I have been influenced by the contemporary example offered by Rheinberger's case study of research into protein synthesis between 1947 and 1962 (Rheinberger 1997). He employs what he calls a 'non-anticipatory' approach (Rheinberger 1997: 2) to describe the small-scale contingencies involved in generating the relevant scientific objects, tracing step-by-step the major shift that takes place between biochemists, who investigated the making of proteins using extracts from disassembled living cells, and molecular geneticists, who thought in terms of information transfer and for whom protein synthesis was the expression of a genetic code. This is a movement from one distinct world of thought and approach to another. At the same time, Rheinberger reflects on the concepts needed, both on the part of the scientists and of the historian, to pursue this business of historical recounting, concepts which are necessary to be true to the materials. In this way, he reproduces the mutual exchanges that took place between material things – the objects of the research – and the ideas that played their part in the complex business of construction and evaluation. I will briefly outline the components of Rheinberger's model, for it offers some concepts to assist our investigation.

First, he sees the objects of research as being produced within what he calls 'experimental systems'. Experimental systems are the working units of research, within which 'the scientific objects and the technological conditions of their production are inextricably interconnected'. And this is not a formal correspondence, of equipment and object of study, but includes the 'local, individual, social, institutional, technical, instrumental, and, above all, epistemic' dimensions of the social setting. We are interested, then, less in the actors' ideas and conscious interests – their 'theories' – than with the things they make and handle and the unconscious desires and motives that work through them. This is a sociological rather than a history of ideas approach and works from the bottom up rather than taking any high overview.

Then, in this perspective, experimental systems generate novelties; they continually shape and reshape their objects, which Rheinberger terms 'epistemic things', but which equally might be called 'images', social facts that show characteristics both of being real and ideal, that are both material and imaginary. The focus is how experimental systems create these new things and how, instead of mapping the known, 'the generation of differences becomes the reproductive driving force of the whole experimental machinery' (Rheinberger 1997: 3) and the mark of a scientific investigation. We might observe that the task of a successful security operation – as we shall see, Ruppelt worked as part of a technical intelligence unit – is not the generation of novelty but rather its mastery. An intelligence operation is created to investigate and explore a new object with the aim of mapping it against what is known and suppressing the threat it offers, as well as, in due course, helping to transfer this understanding so that the ideas discovered can be developed and applied by the home military-industrial establishment. Nevertheless, the apprehension of differences and the development of technical means to that end is the central business of the project, and it will be subject to 'shifts and displacements within the investigative process' in an identical fashion to any good research programme.

Third, a major part of the work of experimental systems, as they generate differences through a sequence of repeated investigations, is that they develop new means of representation: new equipment, first of all, producing new traces, records and statistics. These forms are subject to manipulation; they are material traces which are 'produced, articulated, and disconnected, and are placed, displaced, and replaced' (Rheinberger 1997: 3). We might elaborate: the results produced are detached from their initial context and put to work; they are juxtaposed to other results and begin to generate novelties on their own account and, because they possess an internal logic, they gain autonomy in their working, producing both insights that 'belong' to nobody and automatisms, forms that do not derive from their original context and may mislead. The investigators 'think within such spaces of representation', which are created by bringing together forms of recording – writings, displays, tables and graphs. Creating equipment capable of recording, storing and transmitting information is then an essential component of producing new images and developing existing ones. We are dealing in phenomena that are actively written into existence.

Last, beyond the kind of object they produce and the means by which such objects are realized, experimental systems get linked into wider ensembles or experimental cultures. These acts of linking work by 'conjunctures and bifurcations', in Rheinberger's terms; essentially, acts of comparison. The point here is to emphasize the importance of the bottom-up approach: wider research communities are shifted and coalesce in new forms around the 'unprecedented and unanticipated events' to which experimental systems give rise. Funding priorities and even disciplinary boundaries, despite their appearance of power and their inertia, are organized around these moments of condensation at the local level. And, reversing the perspective, each experimental system has a zone of social impact where its effects are felt.

In short, we are offered four components: experimental systems, images (or epistemic things), spaces of representation, and the wider experimental cultures in which each system is an actor. In the history with which we are concerned, the early Project Blue Book, when Ruppelt was in charge, may be identified as an experimental system, for he created a number of means of representation through a variety of projects, reports, classifications and commissioning new equipment. It is through these means that events – sightings – were realized and reached other social levels, gaining cultural and even political impact. To these four components we should then add a fifth term, that of a 'technical object', when the constructed image becomes something that can be handled routinely and put to work in other settings; that is part of the image's later history.

Hence, we are concerned with 'a record of the process of [things] coming into existence' (Rheinberger 1997: 4) and (as already remarked) not so much with the life of concepts as with that of material traces. In such a history, to return to the gist of our earlier remarks, we are faced with the problem of recurrence, for, at each chronological stage, the relationship between what is true and what is false, what is fact and what is artefact, is recast. For any new addition, anything added to the system, reconfigures the whole, so that each new trace, every new recording, potentially alters the meaning of past results and raises new implications for future activity. For this reason, although we follow a chronological approach so as to avoid reading later concepts back into earlier materials, we are in practice dealing in a systematic description of a 'discursive' object, where shifts in reading and alterations in time perspective – repeated recovery of the past and the present effects of future states – are part of the story.

Discussion

Before introducing Ruppelt, we may wonder whether it is justified to compare his approach to flying saucers with a scientific project. The new objects of investigation – UFOs – display formal properties shared in general by twentieth century scientific research objects: they are simultaneously empirical and rational, concrete and abstract, found in nature in some regard and yet constructed by the investigator. Contemporary scientific research and intelligence work alike play on a dialectical relation between (collective) human reflection and empirical study, working to discern new things and therefore in a different 'dimension' to philosophical representations which seek to map novelty in terms of what is already known. But is that enough?

The biological sciences have to work with multiple variables embedded in complex systems and so, in this regard, parallel the problems of intelligence work. Nonetheless, there is a distinction to be made, hinted at above, between the research of natural scientists conducted in laboratories and the pragmatic questions to be answered by the military intelligence community, made up largely of engineers. Certainly, Ruppelt recognized a difference and was keen to involve university and industry-based scientists, both to gain access to skills lacking in the Air Force and to help resolve local conflicts in the military attitude to flying saucers on an objective basis.

R. V. Jones, both a physicist and an intelligence officer,[2] offers some pointers on the relations between scientific research and technical intelligence work in the period. In practice, he struggles to separate intelligence work from that of pure research. On the one hand, he suggests that intelligence work is 'parasitic' because you are seeking to discover what someone else, on the other side, has already achieved. One is only catching up with matters enemy technologists have already worked out. On the other hand, real discoveries may emerge, when you must contradict the opinions of your own scientific experts; he offers the instances of the bending of radio waves around the Earth and the range of rocket flight, both ruled out by *a priori* scientific reasoning but asserted by intelligence sources and confirmed by experience. Therefore, he suggests, 'the methods ... used in gathering and collating information were much the same in principle as those employed in pure science' (Jones 1978: 529). Furthermore, there are moments of genuine creativity, when new means of gathering intelligence and methods of its coordination are created, and the results synthesized into 'a comprehensively reliable estimate of enemy intentions'.

Jones' struggles come from a common-sense empiricist view that the scientist finds natural objects in the world, to be studied objectively, and he therefore plays down knowledge that bears the marks of human mediation,

---

2   He was Head of Scientific Intelligence on Britain's Air Staff and Scientific Advisor to MI6, 1939–1946.

marking up only moments of originality or creativity. For this reason, he defines intelligence work as being 'on a lower plane of difficulty than research in pure science'. Yet it is not clear that any scientific research in the period discovers its objects in nature; all of them bear the marks of human activity in their construction; an appeal to occasional creativity simply obscures this common quality. Clearly the primacy of human intentions behind the phenomena concerned was crucial. But perhaps the real distinction between intelligence work and scientific research lies in the realm of practical judgement: the particularity of intelligence work lies in the acute need to evaluate risk and to eschew speculation, and in the ends to which that knowledge is put.[3]

The importance of Ruppelt is that he brought the urgent application of scientific methods developed in intelligence work in the Second War and then the Korean War to bear on the problem of what became known as Unidentified Flying Objects. The question of intentionality was present in both contexts, and clearly is differently focussed than in the case of biological investigations. But the concentrated use of scientific methods, the development of an experimental system, was pertinent. Flying saucers were caught up in a short-lived pursuit by Intelligence of sources of scientific information; this pursuit had its own fluctuations of intensity (which we will trace), and the object at issue developed and altered during this process, being lent substance by the various techniques employed. And their characteristics as 'mixed' objects, as images, persisted. The notion of UFOs then took on a life of its own, generating a series of traces and effects – documents, struggles over interpretation, flaps, budget items, career ups and downs, journalistic outputs, new fates for various actors (all of which we shall meet) – without ever being resolved into either straightforward objects or distinct ideas. As with any 'epistemic thing', it was neither left unchanged nor granted a long lifespan in its early form. But this kind of

---

3 When Jones comes to the topic of flying saucers in their early form, the Swedish rockets, and therefore to the possibility of other minds, he is characteristically cautious, and puts the incidents down to the misinterpretation of natural phenomena by people under strain; his comments as always are informed and pertinent (Jones 1978: 510–513).

production is true of any socially constructed object, which then bears traces of its history in the representations it lends itself to.

Introducing Ruppelt

Edward Ruppelt was born in Ohio in 1923 and joined up as an American Army Air Force officer in 1943, flying operations as a bombardier and radar officer in B29 bombers in India, China and the Pacific. After the War he worked in the aircraft industry and went to college, gaining a degree in aeronautical engineering while remaining in the Air Force Reserve. He was recalled to active service in January 1951 in the context of the Korean War, which began in June 1950. On his recall, he was 'assigned to the Air Technical Intelligence Center at Wright-Patterson Air Force Base, in Dayton Ohio. ATIC is responsible for keeping track of all foreign aircraft and guided missiles. ATIC also had the UFO project' (Ruppelt 2011: 7).

The Air Force had established a group called Project Sign in 1947 to investigate and analyse all flying saucer reports; by 1950, this project, renamed Project Grudge, was effectively inactive (Ruppelt 2011: 6). However, at that time, what had hither-to been unsupported eye-witness reports of flying saucers were being corroborated by sightings on radar systems newly deployed for home defence. Early in 1951, the Director of Intelligence for the Air Force, Major General Cabell, asked for a report on the flying saucer situation because of these radar sightings, and Ruppelt was given the job of reviewing past reports by his commanding officer at ATIC.

Ruppelt made his report to Cabell's successor, Major General Samford, and Air Technical Intelligence Center (ATIC) was asked to set up a 'new project for the investigation and analysis of UFO reports' (Ruppelt 2011: 7). As author of the initial review, Ruppelt was given this task and organized what in due course became Project Blue Book, heading the project for eighteen months from 1951 to 1953. He left the Air Force in 1953 (Ruppelt 2011: 232) and produced his account of that time, *The Report on Unidentified Flying Objects*, in 1956; it was republished in 1960 with three additional chapters. Ruppelt died in 1960 at the age of 37.

Ruppelt's *Report* is intelligently written and displays several virtues. In the first place, he had a historian's eye for documents, tracking the memos, reports, records of meetings and official decisions which in practice organize intelligence work in a large social body such as the Air Force. Then, he was a technological optimist: he had a knowledge of and engagement with the new technologies coming online with the Air Force and believed that their use would allow the problem which flying saucers represented to be resolved. Further, he was not simply an organization man and an engineer; through his responsibilities, he gained experience of the interplay between the Air Force and other social actors, including industrialists, politicians, other security operations, and the press; he documented interactions with the media and offered hints about the presence and influence of the other players, within permitted bounds. And, perhaps best of all from the reader's point of view, he wrote well about such imponderables as the workings of a military hierarchy outside the context of the total warfare which had marked its recent past, the changes in 'atmosphere' which governed decision-making, and the political conflicts in interpretation and policy which lay behind these changes. In a sense, changes in atmosphere form the topic of this essay; those moments, shared and individual, signalled in the actors by feelings, even a sense of compulsion, when the possibilities inherent in a given situation alter: a moment of precipitation when human identity – made up of knowledge, memory and desire – shifts. This last virtue, this sensitivity, may have arisen in part from his being in the reserve rather than a career officer so that, alongside his intelligence and adroitness, and despite his administrative efficiency and commitment to technological solutions, he offered an informed but critical perspective, to the extent that, on occasion (as we shall see), he could step outside his role altogether and offer another kind of account of the phenomena he was describing.

Ruppelt's book has a wider importance. In the first place, because it is the unique source from the military side on the first appearances of flying saucers, together with the thorough cataloguing it offers of the various Air Force sightings and of the investigations undertaken by Air Force Intelligence in the period, and because of its citing several reports and documents which no longer exist, the book has been a vital source for subsequent histories of the UFO phenomenon, and is thought by some the single most important work for this period of UFO history. It was not subjected to serious criticism by earlier historians (e.g. Jacobs 1975; Peebles 1994), but more recently, since the release of classified documents and the possibility of freedom of information requests, his account has been open to checking, to being supplemented and to correction. Sparks (2001) in particular has subjected Ruppelt to careful revision, claiming many inaccuracies and suggesting he deliberately concealed certain aspects of the history he was recounting, notably hiding incompetence in certain investigations, rivalries with the CIA over the conduct of the Robertson panel which reported in January 1953, and a small number of instances when reliable data had been collected on UFOs.[4] Swords and Powell (2012, drawing on earlier research by Swords) also offer a detailed reading of the period using the newly available sources without taking aim at Ruppelt. I shall rely a good deal on their work in particular to supplement this account at certain points.

One of the issues at stake in these revisions of his narrative and supplementing understanding of the context is the question of whether Ruppelt was an advocate of the reality of UFOs or on the contrary remained unconvinced; he shows considerable skill in appearing to play both sides of the line.[5] His interest to us however lies to the side of this debate, in the detailed account he gives of how the military lent substance to flying saucers through their methods of engagement with them. This is the second point of wider significance. There were two moments to this process of lending substance: first, the flying saucers were written into existence – though always a contested form of existence – through the creation of documents and controversy over reports, and second, they were given form and shape by the employment of technical means for gaining evidence about them. Ruppelt carefully reconstructs the earlier history, during which the first moment occurred, and then details the period when he oversaw the project,

4   Other accounts, such as Hall and Connors (2000), use these new sources without needing to discredit Ruppelt; Sparks (2001) is however a shrewd critic.
5   Clark believes this may have been at the suggestion of his editor or ghost-writer, whom he identifies as Jim Phelan (Clark 2010: 9); Phelan, a journalist on the Longbeach *Press-Telegram*, is mentioned by Ruppelt as a source (Ruppelt 2011: 47).

the moment during which the 'interplanetary vehicle' hypothesis took form and gained traction. Through considering these two moments, we gain a good insight into the material production of the phenomena. I shall examine two incidents, one from each period, which exemplify these acts of definition and construction. In between, I will discuss the interplay of technological innovation and the control of interpretation which is central to understanding this process of production. By the end of the account of the second incident, the properties of the object made to appear have become clear. I will conclude with the closing-down of Ruppelt's phase of Air Force involvement in the story of flying saucers and review the findings that have emerged.

Ruppelt's work then is valuable because he represents a particular moment in both the creation and investigation of flying saucers, and in particular allows us to see the many-sided contribution the Air Force made to this double process of definition and constitution. His task of leading Project Blue Book was a phase in the oscillation between pro- and anti-saucer factions in the Air Force when, temporarily as it turned out, the pro-saucer group gained the upper hand and it appeared possible to take the subject seriously, leading to the exploration and projected development of a series of new technological 'fixes' to allow the objects to be grasped in greater detail. This phase was however overwhelmed by security issues focussing on mass psychology and the potential effects of flying saucers on the population, arising out of fears of the blocking of vital communications networks at a time of crisis. The 'interplanetary hypothesis' had its moment but was effectively ended by the Robertson panel report in 1953. By that time, however, the technologically driven investigations had lent substance to initial rumours, while simultaneously the interests of Security in manipulating public impressions and behaviour fed into wider theories of a cover-up of contacts from beyond this planet. Ruppelt's *Report* allows us to sketch in all the aspects of the Air Force's lasting contribution to the flying saucer phenomenon.

II. The early context and the contribution of later documents

What extra do we learn from Swords about Ruppelt's recruitment and the political climate in which he worked?[6] We need to make some initial remarks concerning our use of Swords' synthesis. First, he does not radically revise the history Ruppelt gives, but rather fills in the details. Ruppelt is cited repeatedly as a source – particularly the unpublished draft which served as a basis for his book – and his telling provides the framework for the early period, identifying significant documents, personalities and turning points. Ruppelt's understanding and focus remain as the scaffolding of the received account, then, as it does more widely in the literature, identifying the topics and their arrangement and also, as significant, allowing any matters left unconsidered to remain in shadow.

Ruppelt's work, however, is not the only reference point framing Swords' history of the early period; another clear influence is Donald Keyhoe, an early critic of Air Force procedure in the matter of investigations into flying saucer sightings, whose perspective and judgements contribute to the recent retelling. This influence is relevant because, despite the careful chronological work and the detail and documentation Swords offers, there is evidence of a certain smoothing out of the history or reading later conclusions back into the earliest materials, as if there was an answer given, waiting to appear.

This is reflected in my second remark, concerning Swords' anachronistic use of certain terms. In particular, he uses the term 'UFO' from the start, although a lot of the history is tracing its rise to prominence and shifting content, and also the term 'Extraterrestrial', although it was first used in late 1960s as a technical term (see Clark 1998: 219). Yet the various candidates for naming the phenomena, implying possible origins for the unidentified objects, and their rise and fall in favour, are part of the evidence of the history being considered. In practice, drawing on the texts Swords presents, the commonest term in the contemporary Air Force documents

---

6   Swords is the author of the chapters concerning American governmental responses to sightings in Swords and Powell (2012).

was 'flying disks', among the government-employed scientists and civilians and military personnel who reported sightings, and 'flying disks' or 'flying saucers' which appeared in press reports. Official documents discussing policy use such terms as 'unidentified phenomena', 'unidentified object', 'unidentified aircraft' and 'unidentified flying object', in lower case. The use of a term denoting a consolidated object, a 'UFO', may depend on the publication of Ruppelt's book in 1956 before it spread among the public, taken as an independent thing, with properties and an origin to be determined. Before that, it was taking form, without distinct properties. Likewise, the use of the term 'Extraterrestrial' takes the endpoint of a long discussion for granted and ignores the formation of what at the time became known as the 'interplanetary hypothesis'.

In short, Swords gives us materials to trace the history of the terms used and the various considerations to which the shifts in terminology bear witness, but he must be read with attention. What, then, can we say about the period of Ruppelt's appointment from this source?

Broad topics

Swords' account identifies a number of recurrent topics in the military and security culture in which early reports of sightings were received. We can list three such areas.

The first concerns conflicts of interest, competition, lack of cooperation or simple failure to communicate between branches of the Armed Services and, in particular, between the Air Force and the Navy. The Air Force became an independent service only in the aftermath of the War, on 26 June 1947, having previously been the Army Air Force (Swords and Powell 2012: 33), and while its component operations and functions were well established, both its internal organization and its profile with regard to the other services had to develop rapidly in this period. The separation was due to the singular role air power had played in winning the war, which also indicated the importance of air-borne weapons in any future military engagements. As Franklin (2008) points out, while the potential for aerial technology to make a decisive contribution to warfare had been anticipated for a hundred years, it was only realized in the 1940s. Given its future significance, the Navy saw the importance of developing their stake not only in aircraft but also in rocket and space satellite research, alongside the claims of the Air Force. Indeed, Swords suggests the Navy 'inspired the idea of the importance of outer space' in the period (Swords and Powell 2012: 9). The Navy therefore had overlapping concerns shared with the Air Force and these common interests contributed to the early story of sightings.

The second topic concerns the continuing development of advanced technologies carried over from the War. These fell under three broad headings: atomic research, missile development, and early warning detection. Various agencies were created to pursue this research and development, which took place at a number of sites. Swords points to atomic energy facilities at Hanford in Washington, Oak Ridge in Tennessee, and a complex of areas in New Mexico, to aero technology and missiles at Wright Patterson AFB [Air Force Base] and Muroc AFB, to the California Aerotech industry more generally, and to White Sands Proving Ground (a naval station), and the rocket technology of Patuxent Naval Base in Maryland (see Swords and Powell 2012: 31). Early warning detection, however, was notable by its absence and need for development; its relevance will emerge later. One of the issues adding urgency to the early sightings was the repeated presence of unidentified objects over these sensitive sites. It is striking that, in the same period, several US military projects were being developed which, if put together, would have many of the characteristics of a flying saucer: research on nuclear propulsion; the development of a nearly noiseless airplane; long-range pilotless flight; the breaking of the sound barrier; the design of a disk-shaped aircraft; and investigation of a means of propulsion for levitating a disk-shaped plane (see Swords 2000: 86–87).

Three further aspects are linked to this topic. One was the business of recovering German and Japanese military technologies after the cessation of fighting (see Samuel 2004). Another was the necessity of saving military-oriented research programmes as much as possible from the consequences of peace: budgetary cuts and the dispersal of experienced scientists and technicians to civilian life. Among the big war-focussed projects being dismantled were the Radiation Laboratory at the Massachusetts Institute of Technology, concerned with radar development, and the Manhattan Project, which had developed atomic weapons. As an example, the Army Air Force worked with an organization for research and development, RAND, created in March 1946 using experts from Douglas and Northrop (Swords and Powell 2012: 9). RAND's first research paper was on an 'Experimental World Circling Space Ship' (Swords and Powell 2012: 10), from which to launch missiles at the Earth (one of a long list of superweapons supposed to end war through one side holding a superior power of destruction – see Franklin 2008). A third aspect was the potential for cooperation between military organizations and the various agencies and research programmes that emerged. A proposal that the Air Force and Navy cooperate over the creation of RAND failed; however, in another instance, the Air Force succeeded in establishing a joint project with Oak Ridge National Laboratory, the Nuclear Energy for Propulsion of Aircraft project (NEPA) (see Swords and Powell 2012: 10).

All this activity was, to turn to the third topic, in the context of a growing rivalry with the Soviet Union, and therefore the development of ever-more complex security concerns. This topic, again, has various strands. Security concerns were the business of a number of agencies, both within and outside the Military. The coordination of intelligence was a recurrent theme in the period, including setting up Joint Committees between branches of the Armed Forces (Swords and Powell 2012: 122), and, outside this frame, the CIA was created from the Central Intelligence Group in November 1947 (Swords and Powell 2012: 26; cf. 182–183 for the formal relations between the CIA and the Military). Within the Air Force, the three basic functions of intelligence – information collection, analysis, and strategy – were handled by separate departments in two organizations: Air Material Command (AMC) (later Air Technical Intelligence Center – ATIC), based at Wright-Patterson AFB, Ohio, was responsible for gathering and coordinating information – collecting and investigating reports – while analysis and strategy were the responsibility of USAF Intelligence, based in the Pentagon in Washington, DC (see Swords and Powell 2012: 48–51). Within the Pentagon, analysis and strategy were carried out by separate branches. With regard to flying saucer reports, as Swords points out, those closer to the reports 'had very few doubts about the concrete reality of the objects', while those concerned with strategy and at a distance from witnesses exhibited more scepticism and, moreover, had a different agenda, being concerned with the effects of sightings and estimating and containing the threats they might represent, rather than entering into any questions about what in fact was being seen.

The reception of early reports

This complex organizational world received reports of flying saucers from June 1947, with many of the witnesses, because of the location of the sightings, being military officers or government-employed scientists. There had been two relevant earlier phenomena. One was 'foo-fighters' (see Swords and Powell 2012: 3–8): coloured spheres or lighted objects seen off-wing by military pilots in the later War years, particularly in the Far East. These sightings anticipated many of the characteristics of flying saucers: they made brief appearances, displayed remarkable manoeuvrability, showed interest in American planes, 'pacing, buzzing, monitoring' them (Swords and Powell 2012: 5), and, in some instances, caused interference with engines. These balls of light seemed to show intentional behaviour and also represented a possible threat, yet investigators of Japanese weaponry after the War found no technology capable of producing these effects (Swords and Powell 2012: 7). The other was the appearance of 'ghost rockets' over Scandinavia in 1946, again provoking considerable interest both in the press and in security circles, in the latter case because of suspicion of Soviet involvement, either testing weapons or for the purpose of unsettling the population. However, despite many cases and reliable witnesses, these incidents produced no evidence and did not lead to any clear conclusions (see Swords and Powell 2012: 12–29).

In all three instances – foo-fighters, ghost rockets, and flying saucers – intelligence concerns presented two faces: on the one hand, the business of collecting the accounts of witnesses and, on the other, the preoccupations of those who had to assess the implications of these reports. Those analysing the risks identified two kinds of threat; the objects might be enemy weapons of a military kind, or they might be for the purposes of waging psychological warfare. Their potential as hostile weaponry was dismissed quite early on; however, the theory of their being possible cases of, first, mass illusion and, second, of mass hysteria and panic, persisted for some time. These were contemporary preoccupations, drawing on the European examples of fascist and socialist convictions leading to the War, seen in the contemporary threat of Communism to national loyalties, and backed up by examples of the power of broadcasting and of advertising, both commercial and political. Within this psychological frame of interpretation, there is a strong distinction made between those who are supposed to use their independent judgement in public affairs and those who borrow the thinking of others, between experts or 'men in the know' on the one hand and the general population on the other (see the discussion in Melley 2012: 155). This distinction is a recurrent figure in discussion of flying saucer sightings; it is, of course, deployed differently by the various groups of actors, each claiming both science and inside information on their side.

This double frame of eyewitnesses and expert interpretation shaped the contribution made by the press and other journalistic investigations. Sightings were often reported in the local press, sometimes being distributed through newswires and reaching the national press. There was also a series of investigative pieces, published in magazines and sometimes leading to books, which, starting from local reports and reviewing the 'classic' incidents, concluded by seeking an explanation of the phenomena, generally assembled under a single heading as 'UFOs' or 'flying saucers' and considered as a single problem. Given their concerns both with gathering reports and deciding a response, Air Force strategy became part of the story, just as the articles became part of the context of their work. The Air Force had the dilemma of how much to cooperate with the investigations – how much access to grant journalists, how much to release reports collected and how much to say about internal policy – and also, on the ground, how much encouragement to give to potential reports. Against a policy of openness, there was pressure to ask the press to assist the agenda of the security services, helping counter public credulity, quieten potential fears and panics, and stifle rumour. Given the dispersed nature of military institutions, with the local AFBs often serving as the initial reporting point, the intelligence gathering operation based as Wright-Patterson, and the analysis and strategy concentrated in the Pentagon, it took a long time to create coordinated practice and agreed guidelines. Given, too, there were differences in attitude to reports in different places and individuals, and that policies developed and changed, with reversals of point of view at different periods as to the benefits of encouraging reports and of cooperating with the press or keeping journalists at a distance, it is unsurprising that what the Air Force knew and discerning the policy behind its actions, not to say speculating about changes in that policy, became a constant feature of the early history. The official response was an essential component in the sequence that led from sighting to recognized 'incident' via reception and the redaction of reports.

It is worth noting that there was a doubling up of this speculative history, for the task of discerning hidden motives and changes in practice became transferred to the imagined policies of interplanetary visitors, mirroring the supposed behaviour of the Air Force. Put at its simplest, there was a recurrent contrast between the internal interest of Air Force security in the flying saucer question and the external face, playing down the possibility of flying saucers, a contrast which played out in the press and other publications.

A last comment: it is worth considering briefly Melley's account of the Cold War origins of the 'covert sphere', for Swords' account indicates that all the elements of the covert sphere were present by the end of the 1940s, rather than being constructed over the next decade. Melley suggests, first, that Cold War security concerns set the shape for current US policy and how it is presented; then, that these representations associate power and secrecy (together with an ideology of masculinity); and, last, that the conditions of knowing created through an engagement with spying and secret activity provide the basis for a great deal of contemporary fiction (see Melley 2012: 111).

By security concerns, Melley means the separation of a public and a secret face of the state, and the knowing disavowal of the second by the first. This knowing disavowal is shared by the public and, indeed, may be the condition of a modern public sphere; in a sense, the knowledge that there are secret state activities that are incompatible with the everyday principles of democratic life – rules of lawful behaviour and accountability, for example – is apparently carried by the citizen as the price for participating in ordinary life. We are in the territory opened up by Kittler. Melley pursues the expression of this 'secret' knowledge in various themes of contemporary literature, both fiction and non-fiction: the notion of brainwashing and the manipulation of minds, the production of falsified pasts, the forging of documents, the possibility of public denial of things known to be true, the role of forgetting and of recovered memory, and the concept of a permanent state of exception and the need for a demonology to justify it. All these themes play around sociological notions of secrets and of memory and forgetting.

It would be possible to read the sequence of flying saucer sightings and their interpretation as a small part of this history and, indeed, as contributing to the shaping of the larger story. We have already touched on the theme of mind control and we shall see the parts played by disappearing documents and recovered memory, for example, as well as play around the unprecedented nature of interplanetary visitors and their potential to act as good or bad spirits, as fairies or demons. And the theme of literal claims that can simultaneously be denied, the coexisting reality and imaginary nature of the objects, is a constant.

I feel, therefore, on the same wavelength as Melley. My caution is that, despite the scholarship and the convincing case he presents of real abuses, Melley is too engaged with literary texts and tends to despair of the possibility of historical reconstruction. At the heart of this reservation, he sees realism and fictitious reconstructions as alternatives which together share the field, even when mixed, rather than as part of a range of contemporary cultural options that are employed under varying conditions. Recognition of this range might allow a different style of reconstruction. His account in the end is less about the covert sphere and more about literature and film as the source of what we think about security agencies and their work with, reciprocally, these fictitious practices projected to a worldview. While he tells us about the influence of fiction on the judgement and work of these agencies, we learn far less about their activity in the round, and we learn almost nothing about the evidence that might fill in this absence.

Let us continue to follow Swords and trace the ups and downs of the early Air Force projects concerning unidentified objects, filling in the detail of the position when Ruppelt was appointed. We shall pay particular attention to the internal documents Swords reproduces.

Before Project Sign

The first formal project was Project Sign, set up on 30 December 1947 as part of Air Material Command (AMC). It was a response to six months of sightings, beginning from the first appearances in late June and early July.[7] These were of immediate interest to the military because they came for the most part not from civilians but from, for example, the United States Weather Bureau at Richmond, Virginia, Air Force personnel in New Mexico and Alabama, and rocket experts at the Naval Research Laboratory at White Sands, New Mexico (see Swords and Powell 2012: 32–35).

A desk at the Air Force Intelligence Collections Division in the Pentagon began receiving and assessing reports in early July and instructed local intelligence operatives to interview witnesses. There are therefore reports from the earliest days. A contemporary press release from Wright-Patterson AFB announced their engineering division was seeking to resolve the mystery of the flying disks, adding they did not think the disks were captured German technology (Swords and Powell 2012: 37). At the same time, a series of press statements came from senior officers and scientists with military associations playing down the possibility that the phenomena were 'real' or the sighting of new weapons being tested.

The officer responsible in the Intelligence Collections Division, Lt Colonel George Garrett, produced a first assessment – an 'Estimate' – for the head of USAF Research and Development on 22 August 1947. This document (reproduced Swords and Powell 2012: 40) refers to 'flying saucers' and focusses on their appearance, size and technical abilities, including speculation concerning the type of propulsion used, all characteristics detailed in subsequent documents. Garrett also asked whether the Air Force

---

7   There were some earlier incidents which were recovered retrospectively (see Swords and Powell 2012: 32–33).

was test-flying any secret project. As these unidentified objects both posed a possible security threat and raised technical questions, the topic was passed from Collections to Analysis within the Pentagon and the reports collected by Garrett were transferred to the engineers at Wright-Patterson.

A group of experts convened at AMC agreed with Garrett's analysis and sent a second, more detailed, Estimate to the Commanding General of the Air Force in the Pentagon, dated 23 September 1947. This document (reproduced Swords and Powell 2012: 476–478), which is called the 'Twining' memo after its signatory, is headed 'AMC Opinion concerning "Flying Disks"'. It states the phenomena are real, not 'visionary or fictitious', and are shaped as disks, and the size of man-made aircraft. It notes their manoeuvrability, rate of climb, and ability to take evasive action with respect to aircraft and radar, and so the possibility of their being controlled 'manually, automatically or remotely'. It lists their properties, their metallic or light-reflecting surface, the absence of any trail, the circular or elliptical shape, flat on the bottom and domed on the top, their ability to fly in formation, usually without making any sound, with a flight speed on the level of above 300 knots. It offers the view that present US technical know-how could produce such a piloted aircraft, with a range of 7,000 miles at subsonic speeds, but that such development would be a lengthy and resource-consuming undertaking. It looks at the possible origins of such machines, either US secret projects or of foreign manufacture, and speculates on the possibility of a new source of propulsion, possibly nuclear. It notes the lack of any conclusive evidence such as crash remains. And it recommends the formation of a project to make a detailed study, to make a report to all interested parties (it gives a list of military, nuclear, scientific and advisory groups), to receive feedback, and then to collect information and to report regularly.

On the basis of this Estimate and two further documents,[8] Swords comments that, by the end of 1947, there appeared to be a consensus that

---

[8] One a detailed request for information to European Command in October 1947 (reproduced Swords and Powell 2012: 479–484), the other a USAF Directorate of Intelligence memorandum (485–491), both summarizing technical research and a series of incidents.

the disks represented something real and that the most likely explanation was thought to be Soviet technology, probably using borrowed German expertise (Swords and Powell 2012: 44). The focus was exclusively on technical detail, particularly on the form of propulsion (based on the apparent absence of fuel tanks and lack of sound or vapour trail) and speculative modelling. The possibility of American secret weapons remained in the background, supported by lack of communication and trust between the Armed Services. And there had been some talk of psychological effects on the American population (see Swords and Powell 2012: 35). But there was no mention of craft coming from another planet.

Project Sign

This was the state of play when Project Sign came into existence. It lasted less than a calendar year, becoming operative on 22 January 1948 (Swords and Powell 2012: 52) and being renamed on 16 December (Swords and Powell 2012: 65) as an emblem of its restricted scope. The factors involved, in ascending order of importance, were, first, interplay between Air Force and Naval interests, second, differences in perspective within Air Force Intelligence between AMC and the Pentagon and, most significant, the promotion by Project Sign (within AMC) of a third candidate to explain flying saucers, turning, beyond the alternatives of American secret weapon or Soviet origins, to the 'interplanetary' hypothesis.

In Swords' account, the year was marked by a series of incidents, three of which stand out in this part of the story, playing a role in developing intelligence theories. The first was the Mantell case on 7 January, which involved the death of a pilot chasing an unidentified object which is now thought to have been a secret high-altitude balloon being tested by the Navy, but which at the time remained without any convincing explanation (Swords and Powell 2012: 51). The death of a pilot was, naturally, of the highest concern to the Air Force. The next was the sighting by a pilot on 1 July of a tight diamond formation of a dozen oval-shaped disks, which 'made a high-speed dive, levelled and made a perfect formation turn, angled upwards at 30 to 40 degrees and accelerated out of sight' (Swords and

Powell 2012: 57–58). While this sighting again was of great interest to the intelligence community at the time, the case file disappeared quite early from the Project's records, so, although its lasting significance is obscure, the problem of its disappearance may be symptomatic of internal differences. The third case to impress was a sighting made on a domestic flight on 24 July by two civilian pilots, Chiles and Whitted, who reported seeing a rocket-shaped object, somewhat like a plane fuselage without wings or tail plane, and with a double row of windows along the side (implying passengers of some kind) (Swords and Powell 2012: 58–61). This incident attracted a good deal of public attention; the pilots were interviewed by AMC investigators who, in Swords' account, regarded this case as critical, in part because neither American nor Soviet technology had any source that could power such a craft. The sighting allowed a former Naval missile engineer to speculate on reconnaissance flights from other planets (see Swords and Powell 2012: 61).

Project Sign set out over the summer and autumn to produce an Estimate on behalf of AMC for the Pentagon. Swords detects tension between Air Force Intelligence in the Pentagon and AMC over the anticipated conclusions of the Estimate, and Air Force Intelligence within the Pentagon undertook to produce an alternative Estimate, in cooperation with the Office of Naval Intelligence. AMC again contacted the Navy, the Army, and the CIA to check there were no development projects which could explain the multiple sightings, and also asked RAND to comment on the possibility of humanly designed spaceships (see Swords and Powell 2012: 58–59). Negative responses to both these enquiries supported their seeking a third candidate. However, the Director of Air Force Intelligence wrote to the Commanding Officer at AMC on 3 November (reproduced Swords and Powell 2012: 64); in the letter, he emphasized there were two alternatives for 'flying objects incidents', domestic or foreign sources, pointed to the security issues implied by such a choice, and ended by raising the need to take some initiative with respect to informing the public. AMC produced a reply dated 8 November, outlining their emerging position; it was drafted by an operative from Project Sign and signed by the Commanding Officer of Intelligence at AMC. The letter (reproduced Swords and Powell

2012: 494–496) is important because no copies of the submitted AMC Estimate survive.

The letter refers at the outset to 'unidentified flying objects' (lower case) and states that it draws on a base of 180 incident reports, supplemented by other reports and further investigations. It offers a brief classification of types of object seen – disks, torpedo- and balloon-shaped objects, and balls of fire. It gives a range of natural explanations, mentioning sightings of man-made objects and of meteorological and astronomical phenomena, and speaking too of a study based at AMC investigating the possibilities of hallucinations, optical illusions, and hoaxes. Beyond these explanations, however, there are reports 'for which no reasonable everyday explanation is available'. It adds the precaution that no physical evidence has been obtained, and that any investigation is therefore on the basis of insufficient data. But it notes further that these phenomena are 'not of domestic origin' (echoing the words of the Pentagon letter) and mentions the technical difficulties these craft pose from an engineering perspective. And it then 'raises the possibility that the reported objects are vehicles from another planet', before adding again that 'evidence to support conclusions about such a possibility are completely lacking'. Furthermore, it adds that the occurrence of incidents has been plotted against 'the approaches to the earth of the planets Mercury, Venus and Mars', noting some correlation which may (nevertheless) be coincidental. Last, it remarks, on the basis of Charles Fort's writings, that 'similar phenomena have been … reported for the last century or more'. The letter offers three concluding remarks. First, observers distinguish the flying objects from aircraft, and there is no conclusive proof that they are aircraft in many cases; further, there will be no direct evidence to establish the precise nature of the flying objects until there is a crash. Second, with regard to the press and public, it is suggested they be told many of the sightings have been identified as man-made objects or astral bodies, and that the unexplained instances will receive 'reasonable explanations'. And last, it promises a technical report on engineering aspects of the objects.

If this was the basis of the Estimate submitted, it was ill-received. There was a meeting of representatives of the various intelligence groups in Washington on 12 November, for which the records remain unavailable.

The independent status of Project Sign was removed, so that operatives in future had to send all cases collected and analyses to the Air Force's intelligence analysis in the Pentagon, as well as to the Office of Naval Intelligence and the Air Force's Scientific Advisory Board. The alternative Estimate produced by the Air Force and Navy intelligence organizations was published on 10 December, defining the organizations' shared attitude to 'flying disks'. The project's name was changed, to Project Grudge, on 16 December. The personnel of Project Sign were dispersed over the next months to other duties – they first produced a final report in February 1949 – leaving only two men to file cases.[9] And Sign's Estimate was ordered to be pulped (for this paragraph, see Swords and Powell 2012: 65).

The alternative Estimate, designated AIR-100-203-79, was entitled 'Analysis of Flying Object Incidents in the U.S.', echoing the heading of the earlier letter from the Pentagon. Like the letter, the report limited explanations to 'only two "reasonable hypotheses": domestic origin, or foreign (Soviet)' (Swords and Powell 2012: 66). In contrast to Project Sign, the report put its emphasis on the aspect of a potential Soviet threat, and this focus created a gap between legitimate but secret security concerns, on the one hand, and any statement that could be made to the press about the unknown nature of the objects being reported, on the other, creating a space into which civilian enquirers could introduce a largely imaginary Air Force preoccupation with flying saucers.

But not entirely imaginary, as we have seen. Where did the minority opinion offered by Project Sign come from? Can we be more precise about its grounds?

---

9 For the final report, see Swords and Powell (2012: 72); Swords notes that, despite having adopted the conclusions required, a RAND report, 'Space Ship Considerations', was attached as an appendix, which speculates on the possibility of civilizations elsewhere and space travel.

III. The Maury Island incident

The best evidence we have for the appearance of the interplanetary hypothesis comes from an incident so transparently disreputable that Swords does not even mention it, though Ruppelt, who, similarly, was not deceived, devotes some pages to a description. This was the Maury Island incident.

When Ruppelt took over Project Grudge in September 1951, one of his first activities was to go through the older files which had been put into storage after the project fell into disrepute, with some of the files being lost. He ordered and studied the files in a fashion that allowed him to reconstruct the earlier history of the Air Force's engagement with flying saucers (Ruppelt 2011: 69, 112), for which he substituted the term 'Unidentified Flying Objects', claiming this as his own coinage (Ruppelt 2011: 1). In the first eight chapters, Ruppelt gives an account of this early history, simultaneously describing the 'incidents' around which any history of UFOs is constructed and mapping the fashion in which intense Air Force interest following the first sightings in June 1947 gave way to indifference and even hostility to the idea of UFOs by the end of 1948, when Project Sign gave way to Project Grudge (Ruppelt 2011: 59).

We will return to the question of fluctuations in enthusiasm later, for it defined the immediate political context in which Ruppelt worked, but for the moment we are concerned with the investigation of the first incidents. He lists three 'classic' sightings in 1948 which served to establish the UFO question: the Mantell incident in January, the Chiles-Whitted incident in July, and what was called the Gorman incident in October, when a pilot in the Air National Guard reported an encounter with a UFO resembling an aerial dogfight (Ruppelt 2011: 31–42). All three play a role in the subsequent literature. But these reports occurred against a background set by the initial sightings, which Ruppelt characterizes as an 'era of confusion.'

The 'first' sighting, from which the phenomenon is dated, occurred on 24 June 1947, when Kenneth Arnold reported having seen 'a string of nine very bright disk-shaped objects' (Ruppelt 2011: 17) flying in the

Mount Rainier area of Washington. This report has been discussed and analysed repeatedly; we shall touch on aspects of the discussion in due course. Arnold's sighting quickly became reported internationally. Within days, other reports of sightings came in from civilians, civil airline pilots and military pilots. In Ruppelt's account, 'the first sighting that really made the Air Force take a deep interest in UFOs occurred on July 8 at Muroc Air Base (now Edwards AFB), the supersecret Air Force test center in the Mojave Desert of California' (Ruppelt 2011: 21), where several pilots and ground staff reported seeing unidentified objects in the air behaving in an anomalous fashion. At this stage, there was intense interest on the part of military intelligence, but no dedicated organization to investigate the new phenomena nor a coherent plan of how to set about investigating them.

This state of high interest was the context for the investigation into the Maury Island incident in July and August 1947. The incident could be interpreted within a standard positivist framework of 'are the flying saucers real or is the report a hoax?' and, although the matter is still disputed by some, the evidence points towards a clear answer. Nevertheless, a good deal of valuable material comes from considering the incident as a case study. I shall begin by outlining Ruppelt's account of the matter.

Ruppelt's account

Ruppelt (2011: 24–27) is circumspect about the Maury Island incident, concealing some identities while outlining the details with characteristic clarity. The story came to the Air Force through intermediaries and therefore after a delay. Lieutenant Frank Brown, an intelligence officer at Hamilton Air Force Base in California, received a call on 31 July 1947 from a man, S, whom he had already met while investigating a previous UFO incident.[10] S claimed to have a lead on another such incident: he had just talked with two patrolmen from Tacoma Harbour on the coast

---

10   We may note that Ruppelt employs the later term 'UFO' in his narrative; we do not know what terms the actors used.

of Washington State who reported having seen six UFOs hovering over their boat, depositing chunks of metal.

Brown and another officer, Captain Davidson, flew within the hour to Tacoma in an Airforce B-25 and met with S in his hotel room. S was accompanied by a friend, a civilian aircraft pilot. S stated that he was there because he had been contacted by a Chicago publisher and paid two hundred dollars to investigate and produce an exclusive story. However, on hearing the story, he had decided to call in the military to take over the investigation. He had also called the patrolmen and asked them to come over to the hotel to tell their story.

The two patrolmen, J and R, gave their story. J was out in his boat with his crew, his son and his son's dog in June 1947, patrolling near Maury Island in Puget Sound, about three miles from Tacoma. It was a grey day with solid cloud cover. Everybody on board saw six objects just under the clouds which approached the boat and stopped about 500 feet above it. They described the objects as 'doughnut-shaped', about 100 feet in diameter with a central hole about 25 feet in diameter, silver coloured, with large portholes around the edge, and silent.

One of the six appeared to be in trouble, for the others circled around it, one coming in and appearing to make contact for a few minutes before separating. While they did this, J took photographs of the manoeuvre. As they separated, there was a noise (a thud) and the UFO spewed out first sheets of light metal and then harder material. Some of this material damaged the boat, injuring the boy and killing the dog. The boat headed for Maury Island while the UFOs left the area at high speed. J collected several chunks of metal from the beach and tried to radio for assistance; the radio however could not operate because of interference. When they returned to Tacoma, J first obtained first aid for his son and then reported to his superior, R, who did not believe his story until he visited the island and saw the waste metal.

J added two further details. Next morning, he received a visit from a stranger who instructed him to forget what he had seen. And the photographs, when developed, showed six objects but were badly fogged, as if the film had been exposed to radiation of some kind. S (the journalist) added an extra detail concerning mysterious callers: the Tacoma newspapers were getting calls from an anonymous source reporting what was known only to S and his friend and the two harbour patrolmen.

Brown and Davidson did not collect any of the metal fragments, but went to McChord AFB, near Tacoma, where their B-25 was parked. They held a conference with the local intelligence officer and took off for their home base, Hamilton. Their conclusion, the McChord intelligence officer later reported, was that they smelt a hoax – hence their shortened interview and refusal to take any of the fragments collected.

The return flight to Hamilton however crashed near Kelso, Washington, and, although the crew and one passenger parachuted to safety, both intelligence officers were killed. The newspapers reported the fact that the officers were carrying a file of classified reports which, Ruppelt acknowledges, was true but had nothing to do with their investigation in Tacoma. The newspapers also hinted that the aircraft had been sabotaged; Ruppelt, however, having read the report, makes clear that the official enquiry attributed the crash to an accident resulting from an engine fire.

Because of these accidental deaths, two conflicting interpretations emerged. On the one hand, the authorities instituted an investigation which covered not only the causes of the crash but also the case which had occasioned the officers' trip. From the report, Ruppelt notes that the harbour men admitted the whole story had been a hoax: they had sent rock fragments to the publisher in Chicago as a joke, saying they had come from a flying saucer. The same publisher had paid S to investigate the case. The harbour men could not produce the fogged photographs, and one of them had been the source of the tip-offs given the Tacoma newspapers. There had been no mysterious warning-off. Moreover, the report added, neither man was a harbour patrolman; rather, they were using their boats to salvage floating lumber from Puget Sound. The journalist and his friend were simply their dupes.

On the other hand, for those advocating the reality of flying saucers, this event had all the markings of a cover-up by the Air Force. If you suppose the sighting to have been genuine, and the plane to have been brought down by either forces from another planet or, possibly, a branch of security, then the witnesses could have been compelled to make up their confession. The government never published all the evidence leading to the official account, nor prosecuted the hoaxers. These features could all be evidence of deliberate concealment of the facts. From the official point of view, the relevant evidence was released once the enquiry was completed, and the decision not to prosecute was eventually taken because the hoax story was taken at face value and was not criminal. But all the public saw was clear evidence of the Air Force's serious engagement with the sighting combined with a refusal on the part of the Service to communicate all they had learned from the incident.

Further details

We learn more from later histories. Jacobs (1975) gives the name of various of the actors: J and R were Harold Dahl and Fred Crisman respectively, and S was Kenneth Arnold, who had made the first flying saucer report a few weeks before. Jacobs, however, who gives only a brief account of the incident, differs from Ruppelt's in one vital respect, apparently drawing on an unpublished thesis.[11] He claims that in response to Arnold's phone call, 'the army immediately dispatched two officers ... But the interviews never took place because the two army men were killed in a plane crash en route to Washington' (Jacobs 1975: 38).[12]

Peebles' chronicle, published in 1994, which follows Ruppelt closely for the early years, offers quite a lot more detail, including identifying the Chicago publisher, who was Ray Palmer. Palmer welcomed the advent of flying saucers in the October 1947 issue of *Amazing Stories*: sightings of supersonic vessels of non-human origin, whether from space or from the caves, offered evidence confirming aspects of what was called the 'Shaver mystery', a popular series of stories being published in the magazine. Palmer had received the letter from Crisman and Dahl in July in which they claimed to have seen flying saucers and to have fragments from one of them. He knew of Crisman, who had had a letter published a year before in *Amazing Stories* (June 1946) in which he claimed to have encountered

---

11 Johnson (1950), cited Jacobs (1975: 398).
12 This event is prior to the separation of the Air Force from the Army.

'deros' – underground creatures, part of Shaver's narrative – during his war service (letter cited in part by Keel 2014: 121). Palmer was also already in correspondence with Kenneth Arnold over his 24 June sighting of an echelon of flying saucers and asked him to investigate the story. Arnold then met several times with Crisman and Dahl concerning Dahl's encounter, which was supposed to have occurred on 21 June (therefore prior to Arnold's sighting).

In Peeble's retelling, the objects are neatly described as 'spherical with flattened tops and bottoms, a hole in the center, and large portholes along their rims' (Peebles 1994: 13). Dahl beached his boat on Maury Island when they appeared, and began taking pictures; otherwise, the details are the same as in Ruppelt's account. Although Crisman did not initially believe the reported source of the damage to the boat, when he went over to the island next day he examined the considerable debris left and, while he did so, 'another of the objects flew out of a cloud'. Dahl's account of a mysterious stranger is also filled in: a man 'wearing a black suit who drove a 1947 Buick Sedan' warned Dahl not to discuss his experience with anybody, backed by vague threats to his welfare and that of his family. Arnold and his colleague, a civil airline pilot named Captain E. J. Smith, also examined what looked like larval rock and scrap aluminium, and then called in the intelligence officers.

After the crash, the *Tacoma Times* carried the headline 'Sabotage hinted in Crash of Army Bomber at Kelso', reporting that the B-25 'had been sabotaged or "shot down" to prevent shipment of flying disk fragments', and that the craft had been carrying classified material (cited Peebles 1994: 14). Peebles concludes that, 'in retrospect, the newspaper publicity about the B-25 crash was the first to give a sinister air to the flying saucer myth. The talk of "sabotage", "mysterious stranger", and "classified material" gave it a "conspiratorial" atmosphere' (Peebles 1994: 14–15), though the conspiracy was not yet well defined.

Despite not mentioning the incident, Swords adds some useful details. Brown had previously interviewed both Arnold after his sighting and Smith, whose sighting at Emmett, Idaho, had also made the national news (Swords and Powell 2012: 36, 38). Brown was acting as a local Air Force intelligence operative, carrying out instructions from the Pentagon

Collections desk. The incident brought together in a single nexus Palmer, *Amazing Stories* and the Shaver mystery, the actors in two of the earliest civilian sightings which had featured in both the local and national press, and Air Force intelligence operations at both the local and the national level. In this regard, it is a perfect instance.[13] It is important to add, it is not necessary to see this specific concatenation of actors as in any sense crucial; had the incident not occurred, the same assemblage of elements would likely have emerged in some other form. Nor is it necessary to see this particular, contingent event as the original point from which later developments grew; it is simply an example for which we have the details, an example of the production of an ill-defined image, capable of being worked on and given substance.

Discussion

What can we learn from this affair?

First, the story was brokered through a chain of intermediaries: although there was a gesture towards 'evidence', there was no immediate encounter, but simply the report of one, constructed over time by the witnesses, the publisher, his agent and a colleague, and a contact in Air Force intelligence. This is a collaborative venture, with other people waiting to play a part – the local intelligence officer and the press in particular – as the story develops. We are in a characteristic situation where claims are made and evaluated, and counterclaims offered and, in their turn, contested, and the various interpretations and differences presented in press reports and other writings which employ a restricted range of possibilities and roles in their representations.

The dominant characteristic of these claims may be their 'rhetorical' nature, for they aim to establish conviction and persuade the listener or reader of the truth of what is being put forward. To this end, efforts were made to establish the reliable character of the witnesses, and so to evaluate

---

13   I discuss Palmer and the Shaver mystery in the second essay, *Religion and Science Fiction*.

the sense of conviction with which they experienced the contested event, and in this way to create common ground for the belief between the speaker and the hearer, setting out a reasonable narrative. The claims are presented as descriptions, but their task is performative.

We might here contrast the public fate of the testimonies of Arnold, on the one hand, and of Dahl and Crisman, on the other. With respect to character, much was made of Arnold's reliability and reputation in the original investigation of his report in the press and by the official who interviewed him (carried out by Brown); biographical accounts emphasize his hard work to establish himself as a businessman during the depression years, his early engagement with flying, and his youthful sporting achievements. These qualities support his reactions when confronted with the sighting; the emotions experienced can be shared – an experienced pilot taking measurements and making calculations concerning objects of a kind he knew he had never seen before. And the back story he proposed was minimal: he offered no theory, simply a report, and quickly came to distain the kind of attention his testimony attracted in terms of disbelief.

With respect to the last point, Crisman and Dahl illustrate the lesson that the more detailed offered, the less convincing the narrative. The Maury Island incident included too much detail, including offers of evidence which subsequently proved little – the fogged photographs, which were then lost; the materials spewed out from the UFO, which could be analysed and found to be identical to larval rock and aircraft aluminium. The reported reactions and behaviour of the participants similarly lacked plausibility: landing the boat beneath the saucers and taking photographs instead of seeking cover appears unlikely behaviour. And the characters Crisman and Dahl established contrasts with Arnold's reliability: they appeared evasive and finally confessed to having made up the story. Even Crisman's earlier history, glimpsed in the encounter with deros, contrasts with Arnold's life of endeavour and achievement. The one savours of a realistic, technical world that can be shared, the other seems to derive from the world of pulp science fiction. We might notice that, in Ruppelt's account, Arnold and Smith were not told of Crisman and Dahl's hoax to spare them humiliation; their sincerity was assumed.

Second, these worlds are, however, more mixed together than might at first appear. Arnold's role in particular would benefit from more information. None of the biographical material, for instance, gives anything on Arnold's youthful reading or whether he was involved in any fan circles. However, at least since he had made his sighting, he had pursued an active interest in other flying saucer reports, while his colleague, Captain Smith, had recently seen five objects while on a commercial flight. Arnold had been quickly contacted by Palmer and had agreed to investigate the Maury Island incident for him, and they maintained contact, for Palmer published Arnold's account of his original sighting in the first issue of *FATE* in 1948, and they published a book together, *The Coming of the Saucers*, in 1952 (Arnold and Palmer 1952).

Moreover, in a later interview, Arnold claimed to have had sightings of UFOs on several other occasions, to have photographed them on two occasions, and to have investigated hundreds of cases. He also showed traces of a more paranoid frame of interpretation, speaking of the military cutting frames out of a film he had taken of two UFOs that flew under his plane, suggesting that pilots, military and civil, had been silenced by threats from speaking publicly about their sightings, and claiming that his phone lines had been tapped. Last, he spoke of the discovery of UFOs as 'the greatest discovery of consciousness in the world', he was convinced that the Maury Island incident was not a hoax, and he suspected that UFOs might have read his mind.[14] These remarks indicate considerable insight into metaphysical perspectives.

In short, although Arnold is presented as a simple and reliable witness to something new, there also is evidence that he was an active participant in the developing phenomenon, and at the very least, that he moved from one role to the other. It was a life-changing moment. In other words, the moment of experience, the sighting, at least had a good deal of post-hoc work of construction put into it, and we simply do not have any evidence as to whether there was much preparatory work as well in Arnold's individual case.

14   See three telephone interviews with Arnold by Bob Pratt – <ufoevidence.org/documents/doc1998.html> – accessed 3 November 2016.

In this regard, Arnold plays a role in some regards parallel to that of the Fox sisters in the appearance of Spiritualism one hundred years before: he appears to have precipitated a phenomenon waiting to happen (cf. Braude 1989), and to have participated in – but not by any means to have controlled – subsequent events. There may also be a further parallel in the possibility that his founding sighting might have been based on a mistake, just as the Fox sisters later claimed to have been playing tricks. A single illustration from discussion of Arnold's case, a proposed candidate – pelicans gliding on thermals – can produce many of the effects he describes in the article – the shape of the objects, their characteristic motion, the reflected flashes of sunlight that drew his attention – and offers a rationale for his supposed miscalculation of distances and speeds.[15] These and comparable matters are much discussed and disputed on the Internet. However, just as with the spiritualist case, casting doubt on the authenticity of the earliest instances cannot explain either their timeliness or the mechanisms of the social movement that resulted or that movement's success; questions of intelligibility lie elsewhere than in the positivist bathos of 'it was a flight of birds'.

Arnold and Smith are examples of people who are caught up in a hard-to-define process of becoming something new. We might put it in this way: these new technical objects (now called UFOs) call their attention and they respond, forming alliances of a kind with these objects and in this way gaining new properties. There are other kinds of reaction possible: you could make up stories about them, or be sceptical and demand clear evidence, but in these cases, the non-participants are still affected, being brought into disrepute and investigated on the one hand and being frustrated and having their time wasted on the other. The flying saucers distribute roles and rewards. In Arnold's case, participation led to new understanding about the world and its potential ('the greatest discovery of consciousness'), with new objectives, in the sense of knowing what is important, and, perhaps, new allies and new powers: it may be possible to

---

15 <badufos.blogspot.com/2016/08/Kenneth-arnold-and-pelicans.html> – accessed 3 November 2016; this article has a link to the Bob Pratt interviews.

gain new capacities from these allies, powers of thought transference and mind reading, for example.

It is worth remarking that, in this early period, only the circle around Palmer entertained the notion of non-human technologies. In Ruppelt's view, the Air Force was concerned with security issues and with whether they were seeing either Russian weapons, products of captured German war technology, or possibly some secret weapon being developed by a rival service, the Navy (Ruppelt: 2011: 22–23). Swords' more recent research confirms this view, as we have seen. There clearly were minority opinions present in the Air Force, but they did not carry much weight. Given that the security issues were not the solution, however, the outsiders' views controlled much of the action; the more powerful party, despite appearances, were only bit players and caught up in scripts and contingencies not of their own making.

Third, if we turn to Crisman and Dahl's narrative, it has all the markings of a pulp fiction story, notably in its filmic or visual quality: objects arrive which are recognizable, being round with portholes, and show stereotyped behaviour, making no noise, hovering, and then zooming off at speed. In this case, they seem to ignore the human bystanders. A reason is given for their appearance: they have come (near) to land to effect repairs. As they complete this work, one of the witnesses is hurt and an animal killed. Pieces of the humans' modern technology fail to work in their presence: the radio suffers interference, and the photographs are fogged (but note that the boat's steering, for example, does not fail; flying saucers only affect new technologies). The initial response to testimony of the sighting is disbelief on the part of the supervisor, followed by subsequent conviction. A second response, however, is a warning to keep silent from a mysterious stranger in a dark suit and a new car, and an equally mysterious caller to the local newspaper indicates that the witnesses are being continually monitored and overheard. Although this is the first appearance in print of what will be called 'the men in black', all the other elements are already familiar from fiction.

Fourth, however, other effects impinge: the story interacts with real life in a variety of ways. In part, flying saucers were taken seriously by the Air Force because of their reported technical performance: their ability to hover, to accelerate or decelerate instantaneously, to change course abruptly, even to appear and disappear, all suggested the development of a technology quite different to anything known at that time. Similarly, the silent means of propulsion pointed to radical innovation. The manoeuvrability of the craft also posed questions about the kind of biological bodies that could withstand such stresses. Other features mimicked contemporary technologies, with the need for repairs and effects that could be attributed to radiation and electrical interference, and others again echoing practices of the security services, with monitoring and anonymous visits. All these features pointed to real concerns.

In the Maury Island incident, everything changed once the intelligence officers were killed in a plane crash returning from what was, from their point of view, a sterile enquiry. On the one hand, an official enquiry was set in motion to determine the causes of the crash, and this enquiry included investigation of the reasons for the dead men's presence in Tacoma. Unsurprisingly, Crisman and Dahl confessed to a hoax that got out of hand, an attempt to create the kind of story Palmer wanted. No charges followed; at the same time, the security services took a poor view of Palmer's part in the story. There is a striking phrase, in an FBI memorandum from October 1947, that 'It is possible … that the entire flying disk theory was conceived by Palmer and Shaver' (see Toronto 2013: 158–160; the phrase cited 159).

On the other hand, it allowed the interpretative framework already set in place by the pulp milieu to go into overdrive. It started from the premise that the Air Force consistently claimed there was no such thing as a flying saucer but sent highly trained officers across the country at an hour's notice to investigate a report. It continued with the idea that Brown and Davidson, with inside information, realized the significance of the sighting, hence their hurried return to base to report. They were carrying classified documents with them on the flight. The plane had been brought down, presumably by a flying saucer but possibly by rival intelligence interests, and the two men were the target. The authorities investigated but delayed their conclusions, and when they published did not discuss various significant points, nor publish any photographs of the crash. Crisman and Dahl's 'confession' was a convenient lie, and their prosecution avoided to prevent important details coming out. There was a deal of circumstantial evidence for a cover-up and, given the authorities' powers, there would never be anything more.

Concluding remark

I want to suggest the following conclusion from this discussion: in the immediate post War context, the potential of a security threat from an unidentified source meant that science fiction influenced Air Force decisions time and again. It is striking how an informal worldview (with a good deal of justification but, nevertheless, a transcription of life experiences into a global point of view without check or mediation) could at points dominate the workings of a state apparatus. The Air Force could not defend itself effectively from the idea of flying saucers, and this was because it was part of the 'semiotechnical' world which, simultaneously, generated the security threats it guarded against, the means it could deploy to counter these threats, and the means of apprehending this world intellectually, including science fictional accounts to which it had to give answers. It must be remembered, too, that many servicemen would have read science fiction and the pulp magazines; there was no clear boundary between technicians and the public to be drawn in practice.

Because of this mixing, centres of energy and initiative could be created outside the purview of the Air Force and its associated industries, engineering firms, science laboratories and so forth, which caught up and stimulated certain events and frames of interpretation within these formal institutions, creating new directions in research and new possibilities, not simply the putting in place of defensive manoeuvres. Just as in Arnold's case, there may be the taking on of new properties by the institution which were not simply latent but novel, emerging because of the engagement with flying saucers. These new developments would however be quickly covered over by efforts to 'naturalize' the effects of always controversial phenomena, apprehended within apparently stable categories. These developments and their reception are the business of the next two sections: we will look first at efforts within the military-technical milieu to contain these effects and then at the reappearance of such effects with the deployment of a revived technology, radar.

IV. Anticipating public responses

How did the image of interplanetary craft, which had taken form in Project Sign, fare after the correction in an 'anti-saucer' direction, made explicit in the renaming of the group as Project Grudge? I want now to discuss the interplay of two features in the context of Air Force intelligence, the play between technical innovation, on the one hand, and the control of its effects, including its public reception, on the other; in short, the interplay between signs and technologies in the search for unidentified objects. In this way, we can follow (in this section and the next) how the image becomes, in Rheinberger's term, an 'epistemic thing'.

The control of public impressions

Ruppelt offers a sketch of how Air Force intelligence responded to these seductive ideas of flying saucers and sought to control their effects over time, changing quite quickly from keen interest to hostile indifference, which was the state of mind when he joined ATIC. His explanation of this change was that an early commitment to the reality of flying saucers (the memo of 23 September 1947, in response to which Project Sign was set up; see Ruppelt 2011: 16, 59) left too many people in intelligence exposed when no convincing evidence came in; after a year and a half, many former enthusiasts had become critics (Ruppelt 2011: 58, 59). Then (as we have seen), in response to a range of incidents in the first half of 1948, ATIC had produced an 'Estimate of the Situation' in September 1948, reporting sightings, analysing the problem, and concluding that the UFOs were 'interplanetary' (Ruppelt 2011: 41). This Estimate had been sent up the system but was rejected by the Air Force Chief of Staff, who remained unconvinced by the claim; copies of the Estimate were later destroyed (Ruppelt 2011: 45).[16] This rejection had led to a repositioning of opinion among senior staff, and a refocussing of the project. The presuppositions were established that UFOs did not exist and that all sightings were capable of natural explanation, and the task became that of managing public interest so that it died down (see Ruppelt 2011: 59–61). Project Grudge changed its focus from investigating reports to managing public opinion and recommended in what was meant to be a definitive report that its investigative work could be closed (Ruppelt 2011: 68). It is probably noteworthy that, as an engineer, Ruppelt was less concerned with mass psychology than some other players, particularly in security.

One feature, then, of Ruppelt's reconstruction of the early years of UFO investigations concerns the practical business of managing public opinion. This intelligence problem is much of its period, contemporary (as noted) with concerns about mass psychology, whether in the form of the manipulations of advertisers, or fears of brainwashing of captured soldiers in the Korean War, or concerns about political ideologies and the power of demagogues, manifested in the communist witch hunt, or the influence of pulp magazines on teenagers. It is worth remarking that, in an age of advanced technology, the task of Security is not simply confined to guarding against a potential enemy's planes and missiles, but also concerns propaganda, made possible by aspects of the technologies being developed and, further, that this propaganda is as concerned with the manipulation of ideas on the home front as it is with shaping impressions among enemy citizens and sowing misinformation among their leaders.

One example of the desire to shape public opinion comes from the early period of Project Grudge, where the strategy had been from the start to explain every report and to tell the public that the Air Force had solved every sighting, with the objective of putting an end to UFO reports (Ruppelt 2011: 60). Explaining every sighting involved the 'method of residues', a supposedly scientific means of eliminating all false cases to leave

---

16 Sparks, who has searched the declassified documents, notes in a sceptical tone that 'the Top Secret "Estimate of the Situation" of 1948, which concluded that UFOs are interplanetary, has yet to be found' (Sparks 2001: 40).

a core of 'good' instances to be investigated, a method developed in the context of Psychical Research and, earlier, the investigation of Mesmerism (see Barrow 1986). This method however concedes in principle the possibility of there being a residue of unexplained phenomena which can never be fully disposed of; it was not, then, fully adapted to its new purpose.

To help shape public opinion, Project Grudge cooperated with Sidney Shalett, a journalist at the *Saturday Evening Post*, using an Air Force public relations man as an intermediary, enabling him to produce a two-part article (Shalett 1949) putting the new point of view – the first of many such articles using materials supplied by the Air Force, over the use of which it could claim to have had no editorial influence.[17] Shalett's article conveyed the message that most sightings had been solved, offering instances of sightings by high-ranking officers which subsequently turned out to have a natural explanation; that mass psychology explained the interest shown in such reports, giving examples of hoaxes and attributing eccentric views to witnesses; and recasting the history of the Air Force's involvement in the phenomena, portraying the Air Force as having taken on the problem reluctantly because of public disquiet. The Air Force put out a press statement a few days later, apparently independently, again debunking UFOs (see Ruppelt 2011: 61–63).

Ruppelt points out this first engagement with the press was not successful, because the public both believed that people had seen flying saucers and did not understand the motives behind the Air Force's change from interest to disinterest. He further suggests that several reporters began investigations because they believed the Air Force was concealing some new intelligence, indicated by this change in policy (Ruppelt 2011: 64). He does not comment on the fact that it had become an accepted role of intelligence operations to control the perceptions of ordinary citizens, recasting history, interpreting and censoring the present, and seeking to

---

17   Shades of the policy of disavowing the covert sphere in the public space – cf. the brief discussion of Melley (2012), above. Jacobs gives a second example from this period of Air Force cooperation with a journalist to further the shaping of public opinion, Considine's 'The Disgraceful Flying Saucer Hoax' (Considine 1951, cited by Jacobs 1975: 61).

shape future reactions. The means to achieve these ends were the media to hand, print media and radio in the main, employing the kind of evidence that the new technologies were producing in the field – aerial photographs in particular – along with the older rhetorical forms of establishing the reliability of witnesses or discrediting them, sharing the convictions of reliable witnesses, and inducting the reader or listener into a shared world of reasoning.

The two spheres, of media and military equipment, of semiotics on the one hand and technology on the other, cannot be separated, and one can see Ruppelt's stand of 'wait and see' and 'attend to the evidence' (see Ruppelt 2011: 149) as an ethical stance in this context, though one without a clear way forward. On his reading, the task of the Air Force was to protect the nation against potential enemies. He had been brought to the position of having to guard against the possible incursion of machines from outer space. And he wished not to have to take the further step of trying to manipulate the public through putting out partial information, which he also thought to be ineffective. His dilemma illustrates the reality of the epoch which is driven by technology in every aspect, including its self-reflection: because of the powers available to record and, through recording, to generate new 'objects', and because of the ability of technicians to edit recordings of all kinds in fashions which are invisible to the end-user, the world-view given expression by pulp magazine editors and others reproduces many of the features experienced of the contemporary period, features which were not however admitted by positivists nor readily accounted for by teleological models of progress.

A later perspective on the early period

In an earlier article, Swords adds a good deal of detail to Ruppelt's already reconstructed account. He describes a series of fluctuations in terms of whether the pro- or anti-saucer faction had the upper hand over the four years of Projects Sign and Grudge (1947–1951). His guiding theme is that, in the context of the Cold War, security issues rather than scientific ones shaped the encounter with the flying saucer problem, and his larger thesis, that this attitude has continued to influence UFO research to the present (Swords 2000: 83), despite, we may suppose, the change in content of the security worries.

Swords' reconstruction brings out the detail of contemporary concerns about psychological warfare, drawing on the Estimate AIR-100 adopted in November 1948. The earlier wave of ghost rocket sightings over Sweden had been attributed to Soviet weapons and a possible 'war of nerves' and the parallel was drawn with the American situation (Swords 2000: 85). The FBI in this period was asked to look into the motives of those reporting sightings, including political motives indicating communist sympathies (Swords 2000: 88). The Estimate stated that the disks appeared to be real and, in some cases, may be from human sources; some sightings 'might be of Nazi technology up graded by the Soviets' (Swords 2000: 94). The authors' concern was that these advanced machines were being used for the ends of propaganda, to counter the United States' superiority gained from the atom bomb. On this hypothesis, their initial use had been over Sweden during the period when the United States was establishing the eastern border of its economic and political influence; they had subsequently appeared over the United States to cause fear and sow confusion, and to test military capacities to detect and intercept. While they had failed to promote fear in the population, this possibility could resurface if it were learnt they were the products of a Soviet technology far in advance of US military capabilities (Estimate cited by Swords 2000: 95–96).

The view that flying saucers were aircraft was supported by the first combined visual and radar sightings from pilots in Japan (Swords 2000: 96), but since their purpose was supposed to be psychological rather than military warfare, public opinion held the key. The potential of radar sightings to disrupt the psychological warfare thesis was not appreciated at the time.

After the meeting in November 1948, the message changed; from the Grudge report (August 1949), we learn that 'flying disks were errors, hysteria, and even psychopathology or hoaxes (possibly even treasonous ones)' (Swords 2000: 96–97). The frame had been well defined by this stage: we are dealing simultaneously in a possible real object, though with ill-defined properties, and with a range of thoroughly ill-defined individual and mass psychological phenomena, and so with a spectrum of reactions and (possibly malicious) causes that trigger these reactions. The emphasis had shifted from an engineering perspective towards one concerned with managing the mentality of the population.[18]

Nevertheless, the question was not settled by this reversal. The 'negative' period of Project Grudge saw the accumulation of counter-indications to the policy of denial being pursued. Swords gives a somewhat different emphasis to Ruppelt's account of Shalett's article, portraying the story less in terms of the Air Force feeding material to a journalist sympathetic to their aim of playing down public interest in flying saucers and more as their attempt to manage a publication they feared might promote the topic, claiming the Directorate of Intelligence issued a press release to counter some of the statements in the article. While the remnants of Project Sign had contributed an accompanying piece to Shalett's article, nevertheless, Shalett's article was thoroughly sceptical, as Ruppelt notes. Indeed, the Air Force's press release was considered more sympathetic in tone. The confusing messages prompted Donald Keyhoe to identify an Air Force cover-up, first in an article (in *True* magazine), then a book, entitled *The Flying Saucers Are Real* (Keyhoe 1950a, b). The problem identified earlier in the Maury Island incident recurred, of there being material to cover up (because of the fear of psychological warfare, in this instance), but not the material that outsiders suspected (well-based knowledge of interplanetary machines).

Other publications besides Keyhoe's kept the issue in the public eye (Swords cites Heard 1950; Scully 1950), and sightings continued to be reported, notably the theodolite tracking of saucers at White Sands Proving Grounds, also published in *True* by a military scientist (McLaughlin 1950). Moreover, this discussion took place in an increasingly tense context, with, on the international front, the Soviet development of atomic weapons and the consolidation of Communist China, together with the outbreak of the Korean War, and, at home, spy trials and McCarthyism; these were

---

18 Jacobs gives further instances from the period of the use of such terms as 'mass hysteria', 'mass hypnosis' (Jacobs 1975: 41), 'atomic psychosis' (51) and 'psychopathological reporters' (53). We might compare the later shift in interest from physical sightings to recovered memories of abductions.

accompanied by heightened rivalries between the Services for funding (Swords 2000: 100). A series of overlapping consequences followed from this complex situation: the problem of flying saucers could not simply be ignored, for they might give indications of potential Soviet weapons; the Pentagon was answerable to wider public and political pressures; and Air Material Command (AMC) was required to show judicious respect for public observations and reports. In this context, the atmosphere changed, from dismissal to a renewed interest in unidentified objects.

Swords identifies a series of documents that indicate the reappearance of unidentified flying objects on the Air Force agenda. There was an Air Force presentation on the topic (an 'Air Brief Special Study') to the Joint Intelligence Committee, dated 27 April 1949 (Swords and Powell 2012: 76). A letter on the subject of 'unidentified objects' was sent by the Pentagon to AMC on 1 July 1950, asking AMC to reopen the project on "flying saucers" (in inverted commas throughout) and emphasizing the double task of combining collecting intelligence and analysis with controlling any public interest (see Swords and Powell 2012: 101–102). This was followed up by a Pentagon memo of 7 July 1950 (reproduced Swords and Powell 2012: 498–499), balancing the renewed interest from within the Armed Forces with the need to present a reasonable account to the public. This equilibrium reappeared in a document of 18 October 1950 (reproduced Swords and Powell 2012: 500), which again focussed on handling press interest in reports relating to 'unidentified aerial objects'.

The Pentagon indeed ordered the destruction of all copies of the previously adopted Estimate of the Situation AIR-100 in September 1950 (Swords and Powell 2012: 100–101) (though copies of the document have survived), signalling a remarkable reversal in attitude. Yet Project Grudge, situated in AMC, lagged behind the change, producing a series of proforma statements for press releases and responding to reports from the public with statements which dismissed saucers as mythical and of no concern to national security (Swords and Powell 2012: 99); it also continued to reduce its activity and its efficiency, neither investigating nor filing the reports it continued to receive. AMC declared the project closed at the end of 1949, offering a final report (Swords and Powell 2012: 87; cf. 91), although it was technically reopened by the following October in response to the Pentagon's prompting. Swords attributes this lag in part to matters of personality; the Director of AMC in this period had little time for saucers, took an abrasive attitude to reports, and expressed these views readily in interviews.[19]

A shift in focus

In Swords' account, this early Cold War period sets an enduring norm: there was developing public interest, expressed in books and films as well as flying saucer clubs; the military policy combined an appearance of respectful listening to reports with an unannounced strategy of containment and neglect; and there was also a style of academic scepticism which has prevented much serious study of the topic, either at the time or subsequently (Swords 2000: 102). In this regard, Swords contrasts the attitude of engineers and scientists; his view is that the Project Sign team had both talent and expertise, and that they lent towards the hypothesis of the extra-terrestrial origin of flying disks (Swords 2000: 93) in part because of their being engineers rather than scientists (one an aircraft designer, another a nuclear and missiles expert – Swords 2000: 91), seeing problems of design and so forth as resolvable rather than *a priori* impossible or absurd. Although scientists at the time were speculating about new theories of planet formation and the possibility of life 'out there',[20] many also attacked 'pathological' science and 'unscientific' reasoning, assimilating (we may add) flying saucers to occult, that is, theosophical sources. Swords mentions three names of such sceptics: Irving Langmuir, Harlow Shapley and Donald Menzel. The contradictory inputs from the science side supported rival tendencies within the Pentagon of 'possibilists' and 'impossibilists': those who were sure disks existed, whatever their origin turned out to be, and those who regarded them as 'bunk'.[21]

[19] See two articles based on such interviews: Considine (1950), 'Air Force Insists Imagination, Reflections Have Tricked Public', and Considine (1951), 'The Disgraceful Flying Saucer Hoax', mentioned above. Both are cited by Swords, see Swords and Powell (2012: 108, 113).
[20] See Swords (1992).
[21] See Swords (1996).

This was the situation that led to a crisis around what became known as the Fort Monmouth incident, precipitated by the introduction of radar tracking devices (see below) and producing a temporary reversal of fortunes, this time favouring the pro-saucer faction or at least those open to the possibility of interplanetary origins. Several personnel changes took place at the same time, both at the Pentagon and AMC, most of them independent of the meeting where the Director of Intelligence learnt of Project Grudge's inactivity and the Project was reactivated. This was when Ruppelt was brought in to head the unit. It is however noteworthy that when the new Director of Air Force Intelligence (General Samford replacing General Cabell) was briefed on UFOs in January 1952, he was pointed to the security issues – 'Nazi aerotechnology, Soviet rocketry and delivery weapons … [a] possible … novel aircraft with nuclear bombs …' (Swords 2000: 104) – and not to the possibility of interplanetary technology.

At the same time, the Pentagon created the Air Force 'Special Study Group' to identify topics of urgency, and the first question chosen was to ask whether Soviet air and space technology had any relation to UFOs. The conclusion was that these were not Soviet aerospace vehicles, although the possibility was raised that they may be 'artificially contrived light or plasma effects, deliberately manufactured to achieve some possibly psychological goal' (Swords 2000: 105).

Despite this sustained terrestrial focus, which gave the project its legs, under Ruppelt reports of UFOs were treated seriously for about a year. AMC's Intelligence Division was renamed ATIC (Air Technical Intelligence Center) and Project Grudge was reactivated, investigating reports and bringing the files back into order. We may note that, while Ruppelt treated public reports with outward respect, his focus was entirely on military sightings, supported by reports from civilian airline pilots and scientists in government employment (see below). The attitude of the Air Force continued to be constrained by security concerns on the one hand and, on the other, a worry about both the psychological motives of those reporting and the psychological impact of reports on the wider population. The first concern was of course their business; the second, psychological framing, they shared with scientists of the time. Scientists and engineers (among them, the modern military) were held to have a greater understanding of the technological realities controlling life than the ordinary citizen, and psychology, we might say, was the science studying the mental life of those citizens and the social levers available to their rulers or their enemies, another science with practical consequences.

Anomalies arose at the point where military men – pilots – or scientists also saw unidentified objects and, particularly, when these objects were picked up by new technologies. Perhaps the most striking example of such an anomaly occurred in July 1952, with the sightings in Washington, DC. But first we must consider the development of the technology which gave substance to the UFO reports, turning from imaginary play with technical factors to the corresponding shaping of the imagination by technical innovation.

V. Evidence from radar

The anti-saucer 'settlement' fell apart in 1951 with the introduction of radar. There were radar reports of UFOs from 1948 from foreign airbases (see Ruppelt 2011: 45f.), but home reports only began to accumulate in 1951 (Ruppelt 2011: 89, which includes an appraisal of the fallibility of contemporary radar evidence), with the deployment of a domestic defence network in the context of the Cold War. Combined radar/visual sightings transformed the terms of the problem, for a period at least, by offering what were taken to be independent confirmation of human perceptions, objective cross references.

The introduction of a home radar system

Winkler (1997) is the basic source on the deployment of radar within the territory of the United States. Although both fixed and mobile scanners were set up along the West and East coasts of the United States after Pearl Harbour (1941), and civilians mobilized to form a Ground

Observer Corps (Winkler 1997: 11), air defence on the home front was a low war-time priority and, after the War, all air defences were shut down (Winkler 1997: 14). Air Defense Command (ADC) was only re-established in March 1946 in the context of the developing confrontation with the Soviet Union, to 'organize and administer the integrated air defense system of the continental United States' (Winkler 1997: 15). At this point, there were no radars in operation and the available fighter aircraft came from National Guard units.

The focus at this stage was then on planning rather than deployment, and the Douglas Aircraft Company's Research and Development (RAND) Project (later RAND Corporation) was asked to study air defence in 1946. This was in the context of severe military budget cuts immediately after the War ended and, in the heightened competition for resources, with a strategic focus on the offensive delivery of bombs rather than taking defensive measures.

RAND issued a preliminary report in July 1947 which recommended a minimal air defence because the risk of an enemy air attack was considered low. However, the Secretary of Defense announced planning for a national early warning radar network in November 1947, and a blueprint was approved for a radar fence of stations and control centres, to be operational by mid-1953. By the end of 1947 (the first flying saucer reports were made in June), ADC operated only two radar stations, one at Arlington in Washington State, the other at Half Moon Bay near San Francisco. These two stations worked with fighter squadrons to 'perfect ground control and interception techniques' (Winkler 1997: 16), involving the radar detection of incoming aircraft and reporting to a regional control centre, which would alert interceptor aircraft which in turn, once airborne, would be guided by the radar stations against the intruders. These techniques were put to work subsequently by those designing the nationwide system.

In a situation of worsening tension with Soviet Russia, radars were added on the West Coast in March 1948 (with the aim of defending the Atomic Energy Commission plant at Hanford, Washington), and old radar sets were taken out of storage to be deployed in New Jersey and New York State by August. In September of that year, the Air Force added thirteen additional Second War radars to be put into operation over an arc stretching from Maine to Michigan. Together, these comprised the 'Lashup System' (Winkler 1997: 17).

The original blueprint was never implemented because of cost issues, and a second plan for a permanent network to serve as a basis for a credible defence system, made up of fewer radar and control stations, was approved in October 1948 (Winkler 1997: 18). However, the request for funding the new plan was deferred for 1949 and then for the 1950 budget. These delays in turn came under scrutiny at Congressional hearings on weapons procurement in September 1949, connected with Soviet testing of an atomic weapon and with Boeing's moving production of the B-47 from Seattle, Washington, to Wichita, Kansas, on the grounds of the vulnerability of the first location (Winkler 1997: 19). Money was made available for air defence in the 1950 budget, and the first twenty-four radar sites of the revised plan were commissioned in December 1949. These stations covered North-eastern, Midwestern and Western metropolitan regions as well as Atomic Energy Commission sites in Washington and New Mexico. Many of these areas already had temporary radars operating as part of the Lashup System; by mid-1950, forty-four Lashup installations were operating in these strategically important areas.

Winkler also notes that the Ground Observer Corps (GOC) was re-established in 1950, and that by 1951 there were over two hundred thousand volunteers manning some eight thousand posts and making reports. This group 'searching the skies' was only replaced when short range radars resolved the problem of detecting low-flying aircraft; the GOC was de-activated at the end of January 1959 (Winkler 1997: 22).

The outbreak of the Korean War led to an acceleration in building the permanent network, which was completed for the most part by the end of 1951. At the outbreak of that war there were fears that it might lead to wider conflict and the Joint Chiefs of Staff ordered Air Force air defence units to a special alert. This alert uncovered some major weaknesses in the coordination of air defences and led to modifications of the command-and-control structure and the development of identification zones along the boundaries of national airspace. Concerns about air defence also led to the re-establishment of an independent Air Defense Command (ADC) in January 1951, its having been absorbed in an earlier reorganization (in late

1948). These deployments, anxieties and reorganizations provide part of the background for Ruppelt's participation in Project Grudge.

The overall context for the deployment of radar remained a debate about strategy and budgetary priorities: whether to favour air defences or, on the contrary, attack on the enemy as the best form of defence. Approval was given in July 1951 for forty-four mobile radars to protect key Strategic Air Command (SAC) bases (Winkler 1997: 23), but these were slowed by procurement difficulties (Winkler 1997: 24); as of late 1953, not a single mobile radar station was operational (Winkler 1997: 29). At the same time, there was criticism of the potential efficiency of the defence system: a 1950 report claimed that the air defence system would stop only about 10 per cent of an attack (Winkler 1997: 24) and proposed setting up a research laboratory to improve defence solutions. Research led by MIT and shared by IBM developed a computer to speed up the reception and coordination of data from radar stations; work was also undertaken to improve communications and response times. In 1952 there was a call to develop a Distant Early Warning System across the northernmost part of the North American Continent against the threat of InterContinental Ballistic Missiles, and to apply the automation of command and control through the introduction of computers, giving more time for response and interception (Winkler 1997: 26).

In sum, the claims of the advocates of air defence were sustained and strengthened from 1953 onwards, in the face of developing powers of attack and retaliation and in large part because of those powers. In the 1950s, a series of lines of radar defences were built up, supplemented by naval picket ships (leading in due course to AWACS – Airborne Warning and Control System – and Star Wars in the eighties and nineties) and aided by the Ground Observer Corps. Winkler comments that 'bringing together long-range radar, communications, microwave electronics, and digital computer technologies required the largest research and development effort since the Manhattan Project' (Winkler 1997: 32), and points out that IBM gained about half its revenues for the 1950s from this defence related work, giving it commercial and technical pre-eminence in the developing computer industry in the next decade (Winkler 1997: 33).

From our perspective, perhaps the significant fact is that, as the story of the deployment of radar on the continental United States developed, it became separated from the story of flying saucers. Radar sightings only played a leading role in the earliest years.

A series of technological fixes

Having described the (by no means universally shared) anti-UFO attitude which reigned when he joined ATIC (Ruppelt 2011: 84ff.), Ruppelt introduces the incident which effected the change in official attitude (Ruppelt 2011: 91ff.). This was 'a demonstration to a group of visiting brass at the radar school' at the Army Signal Corps, Fort Monmouth, NJ, on 12 September 1951, a demonstration which contingently included a UFO in the tracking, backed up by a later visual sighting and further radar anomalies. This sighting was then in the context of the urgent deployment of a home defence radar network just described.

Because this evidence from the new technical equipment was witnessed by senior staff, a report went not only to ATIC but also to Washington, leading to a request from the office of the Director of Intelligence of the Air Force for an investigation and a report on the incident. A new officer tasked with the responsibilities of Project Grudge, Lieutenant Jerry Cummings, together with his commanding officer, went to Washington (via Fort Monmouth) to report to a high-ranking group including military intelligence, a representative of industrialists, and scientists, and the policy of explaining all sightings as the product of 'hoax, hallucination, and misidentification' (Ruppelt 2011: 93) was reversed. Ruppelt, who was not present, is the only available source for this meeting; he spoke with Cummings, who described the internal politics leading to the Washington meeting as well as the meeting at which he had spoken (see Swords and Powell 2012: 125ff.), and Ruppelt also heard a recording of the meeting which, however, subsequently disappeared (Swords and Powell 2012: 127). He left typed notes of Cummings' account (reproduced Swords and Powell 2012: 501–502) describing the collision between Project Grudge's policy of frank disregard, losing records, and not following up reports, and the Director of Intelligence's need for answers to the 'saucer' question.

At the time, Ruppelt was working at an adjacent desk to Cummings, collecting data on the new Russian MIG-15 fighter encountered in Korea (Ruppelt 2011: 87), and was given responsibility for setting up the renewed project which, in March 1952, was given a higher status and a new name, Project Blue Book (Ruppelt 2011: 131–132).

Ruppelt's experience of intelligence gathering on the MIG-15 is worth comment. We have already drawn attention to R. V. Jones' account of British scientific military intelligence between 1939 and 1945 (Jones 1978), which shows parallels to the kind of problems faced by Air Force intelligence in the early 1950s: the rivalries between the different branches of the services and their intelligence sections, the ability of high-ranked officials to get hold of the wrong end of the stick concerning new items of intelligence, especially during a flap, the contributions from servicemen in the field and civilians which could exacerbate rumours, and the patient work of sifting information and evaluation on which good intelligence depends, sometimes in the face of political and military demands for speedy answers. In the Second World War context, the point was to anticipate the inventions of a hostile nation with an advanced technological sector and to counter them. It was not different in the Cold War. In essence, Ruppelt's story is that of applying standard intelligence-gathering techniques in an age of technological warfare to a non-standard object.

In the case of the new MIG fighter, the procedures were plain enough: the task of intelligence was to assemble and coordinate information from all available sources and to evaluate it in order to gain a picture of the new machine's technical capacities, both to counter its strengths and, if possible, to copy and even improve on the innovations made by Soviet engineers. The relevant information came from pilots' reports, ground sightings, photographs, espionage and reports and documents passed on by resistance movements, and pieces of equipment recovered from combat. The ideal circumstance was to get hold of an entire example, through accident, shooting down, surrender or defection, to be able to examine the various components and their assemblage which together would explain the advantages the new machine displayed.

Ruppelt transferred this approach without reserve (though not without comment – Ruppelt 2011: 28) to understanding UFOs when he took over Project Grudge, starting several initiatives following consultation with scientists and engineers visiting ATIC for other purposes. These advisors pointed to the need for 'reasonably accurate measurements of the speed, altitude, and size of reported UFOs' (Ruppelt 2011: 116), both to eliminate misidentifications and to gain data on the problem. This focus on accurate data lay behind his organization and review of past reports, his commitment to the active investigation of contemporary reports, and his interest in developing and employing new technologies to give substance to the investigations. The emphasis on new technology was in line with the role played by the newly deployed home radar system, which had led to the collapse of the previous 'settlement'. Ruppelt had worked out a plan early in 1952, agreed to by Air Defense Command, for the monitoring and photographing of UFOs by radar units, which would forward the results (in the form of a completed questionnaire) to ATIC, and so to Project Grudge. ADC also agreed a policy of scrambling fighters to intercept any UFO, and the Ground Observer Corps was to be integrated into the UFO reporting net (Ruppelt 2011: 128–129).[22]

He coupled his plans for data gathering with a reversal of policy on press communication. The previous strategy had been to combine a desire to contain and play down reports with the discouragement of public interest in UFOs; Ruppelt advocated being open about the project with the press and the public and encouraging reports. The purpose of the reversal was twofold, to regain public trust and to obtain multiple sightings of incidents, allowing the possibility of triangulation and so of measuring the speed, altitude, and size of UFOs with some accuracy (see Ruppelt 2011: 117).

It is worth noting that Ruppelt put equal weight on radar and visual sightings, rather than favouring exclusive use of the new technologies, although he distrusted civilian reports as compared with those of 'expert' witnesses. This even-handedness is in part because he was clear-sighted

22   It is worth remarking that, in contrast, Project Sign had asked for a newspaper clippings service and for interceptors on standby and had been refused both – see Swords and Powell (2012: 53–54).

about the potential problems of radar sightings in terms of the artefacts created by weather inversions and the possibility of picking up the reflections of objects moving on the ground (see Ruppelt 2011: 89–91).

He made plans, however, to overcome this problem: a series of further technical fixes. With official permission, he made a contract with a research and development corporation named Project Bear in the book (later identified as the Battelle Memorial Institute), to offer the expertise that the Air Force lacked and to develop two projects, the one a psychological 'study of how much a person can be expected to see and remember from a UFO sighting' (Ruppelt 2011: 118), the other a statistical study of UFO reports.

The outcome of the psychological study of the powers of testimony of a witness was to be a practical and realistic questionnaire which could be used to collect reliable data. The purpose of the statistical study was to create 'a complete UFO file on IBM punch cards' (Ruppelt 2011: 118), so that 'the files could be sorted electronically' (Ruppelt 2011: 119) and patterns might be perceived. Put together, the details of the new questionnaire could build up a reliable file of reports which would in turn allow the creation of a 'modus operandi file', 'similar to the M. O. files used by police departments to file the methods of operation of a criminal'. Although the example Ruppelt gives concerns the elimination of cases, the method of residues he proposes would presumably also allow the identification of specific types of UFOs and even of individual craft.

It is worth remarking this process of creating a data base: of producing an object by receiving reports, filling in questionnaires, making file cards, and sorting by computer. It carries the risk that a natural object may be denatured, and also that a set of unrelated incidents may become coordinated and translated into a new instance of intentional behaviour. Yet this apparatus is the adoption of a scientific method, self-consciously generating its own artefacts. In this fashion, the desire to measure (Ruppelt 2011: 116) may serve as a productive intervention in the real world of which it hoped to gain knowledge. I will offer a further comment at the end of this section.

Swords' later analysis of the materials brings out two security concerns that were sensitive but underplayed or absent from Ruppelt's account. First, as we have seen, the idea of mass psychology played an important role at the beginning of the 1950s, together with the possibilities of psychological warfare. A considerable element in security interests concerned the fear that flying saucers were Soviet machines of some kind designed to sow panic among the population and to allow the production of confusion at critical moments, including the temporary overloading and blocking of communications networks, aiding an unannounced air attack. There was a variety of theories as to the means of producing these effects, and various forms of evidence pointed to (for instance, the absence of any official Russian discussion of saucers). The suggestion of 'artificially contrived light or plasma effects' was particularly subtle, for flying saucers behave very like the reflection of sunlight off a watch face on a wall, silent, without a trail, appearing and disappearing in an instant, combining immobility and sudden bursts of impossible speed.

Second, although Ruppelt repeatedly invoked weather balloons, including skyhook balloons, as objects that may have been misidentified as UFOs, there was also a programme developing high flying spy balloons – before the invention of high flying jet aircraft (the U-2) and satellites – and these projects were kept highly secret; one of the advantages of UFO sightings was potentially to distract from accidental glimpses of these objects during testing. Even in security circles, then, repeated denials in answer to the question 'Does the U.S. have a secret weapon that is being reported as a UFO?' (Swords and Powell 2012: 117) were to be expected.

Returning to Ruppelt's innovations, the positive feature of this approach was that there was no credibility gap between the witnesses and the technicians; UFOs were reported from aircraft in flight, caught on radarscopes or, when seen from the ground, seen through theodolites recording missile testing or over other secure sites. The appearance of UFOs around vital defence areas was a matter of comment: 'The Los Alamos-Albuquerque area, Oak Ridge, and White Sands Proving Ground rated high. Port areas, Strategic Air Command bases, and industrial areas ranked next' (Ruppelt 2011: 116); it is not entirely surprising that UFOs were first thought of in terms of Soviet spy missions. Further evidence then came from plotting paths and correlating timings, coordinating reports with information gathered for other practical purposes (about meteorological conditions, the launching of weather and other balloons, and military and civilian flights), and creating statistical analyses of data, only possible with the use of computers. The further proposals to help clear matters up were also engineering projects, the creation of new means of collecting better data. Three such projects were the early 'Operation Twinkle' in 1949, proposing to set up a series of cinetheodolites normally used for recording the trajectory of missiles under test (Ruppelt 2011: 51), the idea in 1952 of deploying flights of aircraft waiting to gain better photographs of UFOs (Ruppelt 2011: 138), and the proposal, also in 1952, to develop a diffraction grating on a long focal-length camera allowing more detailed pictures to be taken (Ruppelt 2011: 149), none of which reached fruition.[23] There was a further proposal in late 1952 for the development of coordinated radar sightings and photographic evidence which also came to nothing (Ruppelt 2011: 198 – see below). The method of residues with its asymptotic approach to presence was to be supplemented by further technical fixes.

Comment

If we take a more distanced view, we began with the wider cultural milieu of military and technical intelligence in the immediate post-War, and saw the disturbances produced by certain anomalous events. The introduction of radar allowed an amalgam of elements created by the earlier ill-defined sightings and their accompanying narratives to precipitate into a 'research object', an object which simultaneously embodies specific concepts. This was identified by a restricted group who developed other instruments and techniques to pursue systematic research into the object, an 'experimental system' in Rheinberger's term. This was Ruppelt's achievement. The work of the experimental system can be described in broad terms as the development of a 'space of representation', using new means of representation, making and ordering reports, creating statistics, building new equipment, creating new 'traces' or inscriptions and manipulating these forms of registration or record. The researchers' thinking took place within this space of representation, which was not stable but, on the contrary, multiple – held

---

23   Except for the diffraction grating, which was later found to be ineffective (Ruppelt 2011: 229).

between various parties – and dynamic, with presuppositions, conventions, means employed and arrangements of elements all developing.

This thought, and the manipulations inseparable from it, has its own logic, which does not belong to the actors. These manipulations give substance to the objects as they assay them, and yet at the same time are constrained by the state of the enquiry and the stimulus of the objects; they seek to discern their objects' inner reasons, set up new means of gaining insight, and plot their hybrid trajectories; in short, there is a dialectic of experimentation and instrumentation (cf. Hacking 1983).

There are three basic moves at the heart of this untidy process, replication (though never repetition), transcription, and translation of information, forming a history of experimental events but never a chronicle (cf. Rheinberger 1997: 7). These are the dimensions in which a scientific object comes into existence, through systematic reiterations which never fully replicate, the comparison of the differences which emerge, and their abstract representation in a sequence of traces, forms which can be interpreted.

In this fashion, singularities become routinized and conventional interpretations developed, only to be overthrown by new circumstances. As the practitioners learn to handle their experimental systems, and what were originally shocks to the system – destroying its temporary coherence and causing new arrangements – become incorporated as parts of practical machinery to allow new observations, the experimental system develops its own intrinsic powers. As Rheinberger observes, the experimental system is not usually well defined, and the system of experiments does not produce clear answers. They only appear transparent and tell a clear story when viewed in retrospect, as a 'dead stretch', with the life and confusion, the discarded hypotheses and intellectual cul-de-sacs, left out of sight. In practice, experimental systems are 'machines for making the future ... systems of manipulation designed to give unknown answers to questions that the experimenters themselves are not yet able clearly to ask' (Rheinberger 1997: 28).

At the same time, the experimental system is not independent of its wider context, either in natural or in human cultural terms, and it may run out of road or come into conflict with some larger force. The complex image that has been developed may be put to work in another context, neither foreseen nor chosen by the original investigators. We now turn to the second formative moment of the early history, the Washington incident and its aftermath, the momentary triumph of the interplanetary hypothesis and its subsequent demise in the Robertson panel report.

VI. The importance of the Washington incident

The story so far concerns the role of hierarchy and opinion in the Air Force and the potentially disruptive part a new technology can play in this context. But two other factors should be considered: the place of the press and the importance to the public of sightings. Ruppelt was aware of the first; he had a liaison officer introduced at the Pentagon to handle enquiries (Ruppelt 2011: 130) and he details the role played by individual press articles in the narrative (Shalett 1949; McLaughlin 1950; Keyhoe 1950a; Ginna 1952). He was less good on the second, tending to rely heavily, as we have noted, on 'reliable' witnesses – military men, civil airline pilots, scientists (usually on government projects), engineers and security specialists – to whom he also turns in his efforts to create better evidence (see his work on measurement and questionnaires – Ruppelt 2011: 116–117). The higher echelons of the Service, mixing with politicians, were however concerned with the effects of press stories on public opinion, and the work of Project Blue Book became effectively controlled by these concerns. This control became clear in the flying saucer 'flap' of June 1952, which culminated in the sighting of flying saucers over Washington in July. In this incident, we can see how the image or 'epistemic thing', carefully constructed and worked up by the various technological projects ordered by the Air Force in Ruppelt's spell at Project Blue Book, escaped its frame and became what Rheinberger calls a 'technical object', an autonomous arrangement with more or less known properties which can be put to work as a component in other systems (see Rheinberger 1997: 28–31).

The June flap

The June flap consisted in an unprecedented number of sightings, equalling or exceeding all previous reports (Ruppelt 2011: 141). It coincided with a move up the organizational chart for Project Blue Book, which 'had risen from the one-man operation to a project within a group, then to a group, and now it was a section' (Ruppelt 2011: 143). This increase in importance marked the Air Force taking the UFO problem seriously, supported by a series of fighter pilot reports and radar sightings from Korea and a coincident rise in radar and visual sightings at home.

There were some 'firsts' in this period: the first radar tracking of a UFO during a climb over Los Angeles (Ruppelt 2011: 143), for example, and the first series of visual reports tracking the same object, rather than isolated sightings, from Virginia (Ruppelt 2011: 144). Reports came from all over the United States, but with a trend building on the East Coast (Ruppelt 2011: 144). Many were open to natural explanation – weather balloons, atmospheric inversions – but reports continued to come in, from official wires and letters from the public, with about a fifth of intelligence officers' reports classified 'unknown' (Ruppelt 2011: 147).

Part of Ruppelt's duties in this period comprised regular briefings in Washington; he reports one such meeting in mid-June which included the Air Force Director of Intelligence (General Samford) and members of his staff, two captains from the Office of Naval Intelligence, and 'some people I can't name', presumably from the security agencies. He put forward the official stance of Project Blue Book, that, despite the good data coming in, there was still no proof that UFOs are anything real (Ruppelt 2011: 148): an open-minded but cautious attitude.

At this meeting, one of General Samford's staff challenged this stance, asking whether, 'if you make a few positive assumptions instead of negative assumptions you can just as easily prove that the UFOs are interplanetary spaceships? Why', he asked, 'do you always pick the assumption that proves that UFOs don't exist?' (Ruppelt 2011: 148). This episode revealed how far there was a split within the leading group in Air Force intelligence, articulated around the question 'Why not simply believe that most people know what they saw?' (Ruppelt 2011: 149). Ruppelt defended the principle of scientific caution until you obtain positive proof, and 'the outcome of the meeting was a directive to take further steps to obtain positive identification of the UFOs' (Ruppelt 2011: 149), in the instance, for ATIC's technical section to develop further equipment (a superior camera with a diffraction grating which could pick up greater detail).

Ruppelt identified the existence of a widespread lobby at this point in the Pentagon, at Air Force Command Head Quarters, on the Research and Development Board and elsewhere in government, who wanted a change in policy: they wanted to know more about UFOs, not whether they existed; they wanted a clamp-down on any release of information, for security reasons; and they wanted to mobilize efforts, drawing scientists into the project (Ruppelt 2011: 152). General Samford however did not alter his policy, drawn up originally by Ruppelt, of waiting for positive evidence. Further reports flooded in, in part because of renewed high-up Air Force interest, and they played into this political situation.

The Washington incident – July 1952

Ruppelt held his cautious views out of conviction, I believe; the story he tells repeatedly is one of Air Force incompetence, not of any conspiracy to conceal, and of the institution's vulnerability in the face of press and political pressure. Although he tells the story dramatically, presenting the puzzles first and leaving explanations until later pages, in practice he offers little evidence for 'unknown' sightings and puts forward a good many natural explanations; his story is rather that he was not allowed the opportunity and resources to conduct a thorough investigation at the time. His tone of exasperation comes more from his falling out of love with the Air Force over this period rather than his feeling that their overall policy was misguided or deceptive. But this is the episode which led to a further reversal of priorities (for reasons very like those behind the first loss of interest) and the permanent relegation of UFOs to a low priority and the status of an embarrassment, from the Air Force point of view, to be rid of; it was simultaneously the high point and the fall of Project Blue Book.

He may well have written the book to explain his professional failure rather than to advocate the existence of UFOs.

With respect to the Washington sightings, there had been a period of preparation, with the June Flap and 'a build-up of reports along the east coast of the United States' (Ruppelt 2011: 157) and discussions of them among official bodies. There was also a lead-in of civilian pilots reporting UFOs, lights for the most part, in the wider area around Washington, and a ground sighting from 'a high-ranking civilian scientist from the National Advisory Committee for Aeronautics Laboratory at Langley AFB'. Each sighting combined some of the elements of silent flight, sudden changes of speed, height and direction, and lights joining and separating.

The Washington sightings involved three radar systems, Washington National Airport's Air Route Traffic Control (ARTC), the short-range radar at the Airport's control tower and, ten miles to the east, the radar at Andrews AFB. Shortly before midnight on 19 July 1952, the National Airport's ARTC radar picked up eight unidentified objects east and south of Andrews AFB, first 'loafing', then accelerating out of radar range (Ruppelt 2011: 158, 159). The operators alerted Andrews; they also asked pilots in the area to keep a look out, some of whom saw 'mysterious lights', which were also reported by control tower operators; other operators, when questioned, had not seen lights (Ruppelt 2011: 160). Jet fighters were brought in but were delayed and turned up after the targets had gone (Ruppelt 2011: 161).

A report was requested from intelligence at Bolling AFB, situated between the National Airport and Andrews. The report, made the next day, stated that the ARTC had checked with the control tower and with Andrews and both had confirmed the targets and their behaviour (Ruppelt 2011: 159). The targets had flown through prohibited areas over the White House and the Capitol (Ruppelt 2011: 160). The three radars later picked up a single target simultaneously for a short duration.

In a later appraisal of the evidence, Ruppelt notes that this was the only occasion when the three systems simultaneously picked up a target, although many targets appeared in the overlap area between the systems (Ruppelt 2011: 170). The ARTC operators checked their equipment and found no malfunction (Ruppelt 2011: 159), but a later suggestion was made that they had picked up targets from the ground. There was also a report of seeing a 'huge fiery-orange sphere' hanging over the range station at Andrews AFB (Ruppelt 2011: 160), but this story was later denied by the operators who had made it, perhaps under pressure (Ruppelt 2011: 169). A testimony from the pilot who had picked up a possible ground target suggested there were so many lights over Washington that you were bound to see a 'mysterious light' (Ruppelt 2011: 170).

In Ruppelt's account, the evidence was inconclusive at best. His story develops around the press reports of this incident and the pressure these created on the Air Force hierarchy, together with the role of lower officialdom.

The initial problem was that throughout the excitement, including calling in fighters, no one had informed Air Force intelligence, who were then unprepared for press questions the next day, leading to headlines of 'The Air Force won't talk' kind (Ruppelt 2011: 158). Ruppelt arrived in Washington on 20 July for a routine meeting and was caught up in the Pentagon intelligence's discussions, with the tasks of containing press interest and avoiding political interventions uppermost (Ruppelt 2011: 161), a day of much talk and no decisions until, late in the day, the press office issued an official 'no comment' pending Ruppelt's investigation of the sightings (Ruppelt 2011: 162).

Ruppelt planned a series of interviews, but then gives an account of his failure to carry these out: he was frustrated first by an official's refusal to put a staff car at his disposal (he was of too low a rank), then by another official's refusal to cover the expenses of the enquiries, and finally by the same official's advice that he had no formal permission to extend his absence from his base in Dayton and that he would be absent without leave. He checked with his senior officer and left Washington without achieving his task, defeated by Air Force red tape (Ruppelt 2011: 162); the various acts of fact-checking mentioned above took the best part of a year to collect, though they could have been completed in the day (Ruppelt 2011: 169).[24]

---

24 Sparks (2001: 46) however challenges more or less every detail of Ruppelt's account, suggesting he was closed out of the investigation by Air Force intelligence personnel and that he wished to conceal this fact in his history of the incident.

The second incident

The second Washington National Airport sighting followed a week later, almost to the hour. Again, nobody thought to inform Air Force intelligence, but a journalist from *Life* magazine rang Ruppelt during the sighting; this early contact resulted in some Pentagon officers being present in the ARTC radar room. The same radar operators picked up the same slow-moving targets, which the tower radar and Andrews AFB also located. Jet interceptors were called out, journalists were excluded from the radar room, and civilian air traffic was kept out of the area. 'But just as the two '94's arrived in the area the targets disappeared from the radarscopes' (Ruppelt 2011: 164–165). The aircraft looked around and then returned to base. A few minutes later, the unidentified targets reappeared on the radar scopes.

In the interval, 'bright lights that were "rotating and giving off alternating colors"' (Ruppelt 2011: 165) were seen around Langley AFB in Virginia, and an F-94 in the area contacted. It started towards the visual target, but the lights extinguished; the F-94 got a radar lock-on, but this 'was broken in a few seconds as the target apparently sped away'. This sequence of lock-on and break was repeated twice.

A few moments after the last break, the targets reappeared on the radarscopes at Washington National. Once again, the traffic controller asked for interceptors, guiding the jets towards targets which, however, sped away as the jets approached or, in one case, disappeared. The jets ran low on fuel and returned to base and, at dawn, minutes later, all the targets had gone.

These targets gave evidence to the radar, appearing as well-defined, solid objects; they could be seen by the pilots as lights; and they had a characteristic pattern of behaviour, being able to loiter at one hundred miles per hour or to out-run a jet, open to being chased but never caught.

These repeat sightings also raised considerable press interest, and sowed confusion at the Pentagon; the President's Air Aide called to find out what was going on (Ruppelt 2011: 166–167). Prior to the Washington sightings, radar and visual sightings rarely coincided. Now there were several instances, including some from further afield; Ruppelt gives a contemporary case from California, once again a game of cat-and-mouse between a UFO and an F-94 (Ruppelt 2011: 167–168).

General Samford held a press conference on the following Tuesday, 29 July. He sustained the official line that the sightings were due to natural phenomena. In Ruppelt's account, Samford was handicapped by the failure of intelligence to provide information, and that was due to the relevant officers having failed to make proper enquiries. Neither Samford nor the radar expert called in had command of all the recent facts, and this could look like a cover-up (Ruppelt 2011: 168); in fact, they were covering for their people, not concealing knowledge of the presence of flying saucers for fear of public panic.[25] Again, a typical pattern emerged, this time in relation to public statements: the Air Force appeared to be reticent about what it knew while insisting that, to the best of its knowledge, there was nothing to know. The press took the message that the official line was natural phenomena but was distrustful of the Air Force's reluctance to give out information. Ruppelt's conclusion was that the lack of information was due to a lack of enquiry, and not to any cover-up (Ruppelt 2011: 169).

Ruppelt sums up the arguments pro and con the significance of the Washington incident in the light of the evidence gradually assembled. Against: there was doubt about the sightings, with too many changed stories; there were too many lights around to identify mystery lights; the radars were probably picking up ground objects, from atmospheric inversions; and there was only a single occasion when an object was picked up simultaneously on the three radars. In favour: there had been more radar sightings and lights over Washington between the two Saturday nights and later, extending into August; then, the weather conditions – of 'inversion' – were constant, but the sightings were not; and the radar operators were experienced technicians, with daily responsibility for thousands of lives (Ruppelt 2011: 170).

25   Ruppelt has in mind Donald Keyhoe's account of the press conference in *Flying Saucers from Outer Space* (Keyhoe 1953) and cites his discussions with Samford at the time against this interpretation. On the other hand, there were repeated references in earlier UFO files to the 1938 panic around the Orson Welles radio dramatization of *The War of the Worlds* – see Ruppelt (2011: 58).

His conclusion is that the Washington sightings remain 'unknowns'. But the incident remains a classic, much cited,[26] for it has all the necessary elements: a building of expectation, delivery of the phenomenon (with a repeat), poor investigation, intense press interest, and involvement of the highest levels of the military and the state.

If Ruppelt undermines the credibility of the Washington sightings, he also simultaneously offers positive evidence for, in a coda to the chapter, he gives another sighting on the same day as the press conference, in this case a 'good' sighting. It took place in Michigan, involving a radar sighting, an interception and visual sighting of a light, and continuous contact between the radar operator and the pilot. The target made a 180-degree turn, and the jet began to follow, got a radar lock-on, and began to close, whereupon the target accelerated away but sustained the chase for ten minutes, allowing repeated closings-in and making escapes, at speeds varying between 1,400 and 200–300 miles an hour (Ruppelt 2011: 171–172). This, Ruppelt claims, is as good a sighting as you will get: 'Even if all of the thousands of other UFO reports could be discarded on a technicality, this one couldn't be' (Ruppelt 2011: 172).

The aftermath of the Washington Incident (a) the apotheosis of the interplanetary hypothesis

The Washington Incident had produced the side-effect that civilian calls had blocked Air Force communications channels for a period of three to four hours. As Swords remarks, 'this swamping of channels was immediately recognized as a national security issue' (Swords 2000: 106). Indeed, the incident as a whole – the surge of reports, the newspaper headlines, the simultaneous visual and radar sightings, and the flying saucers overflying high security areas of the nation's capital – had drawn the attention of the White House, and the pragmatic problem of a breakdown in the Air Force's response mechanisms prompted President Truman to require

---

26   For the detail, see Swords and Powell (2012: 154–163) and Clark (1998: 653–662).

'the CIA to look into the UFO problem, estimate its seriousness, and decide what could be done' (Swords 2000: 108).

At the same time, the pro-UFO forces in the Pentagon appeared to have been vindicated. Although the press conference following the Washington Incident may have had the air of a public relations crisis, as Ruppelt reports, a wider effect was that a number of further initiatives were also being planned. The 'interplanetary hypothesis' had been discussed in both military and scientific circles from early 1952, leading to a proposal to convene a panel of scientists to evaluate the evidence that had been gathered by Project Blue Book (Ruppelt 2011: 199–200). This interest reversed the dominant opinion of a year before, when the topic of spaceships had been responsible for the loss of interest in UFOs within the military. In Ruppelt's view, in part because of this inconstancy, while the Air Force could gather information it had to be evaluated by scientists and engineers (Ruppelt 2011: 200). He therefore put together a preliminary panel of four experts which met in November 1952, and it recommended a full evaluation of the reports gathered, which the Air Force agreed to convene.

There were several potential sources of new evidence. In the first place, Ruppelt discusses a study (initiated in the Pentagon) of the movement of UFOs, 'trying to prove that the motion of a UFO as it flew through the air was intelligently controlled' (Ruppelt 2011: 189). There had been incidents in which 'UFOs made a series of manoeuvres' (Ruppelt 2011: 190) such as repeated turns and constant length runs (Ruppelt 2011: 187–188) and others in which they played a game of cat-and-mouse with aircraft that pursued them (Ruppelt 2011: 171–172). There was also film which appeared to show that a group of UFOs showed ordered motion (behaving like swallows rather than gnats – Ruppelt 2011: 190).

In the second place, Ruppelt thought he had found a source of supplementary evidence in measurements of background radiation (for which data existed from 1949), where an abnormal increase in radiation coincided with a UFO sighting (Ruppelt 2011: 204f.). He believed it would be possible to correlate data from radar, visual sightings, and tracking with measurements of background radiation (Ruppelt 2011: 207). Although this approach looked promising, nevertheless, experts judged the data inconclusive (Ruppelt 2011: 209).

At the same time as bringing together a panel of experts to consider the evidence, Project Blue Book had made plans to attend the testing of the first H-bomb, with the expectation that 'beings, earthly or otherwise' might also turn up to observe (Ruppelt 2011: 197), and sought formal permission to implement an extensive 'planned tracking system', using a variety of instruments to track UFOs, and replacing the diffraction grid camera being developed in response to an earlier decision. Although attending the test did not work out (nor were any interplanetary craft reported), the new senior officer at ATIC backed the plan to develop a series of 'visual spotting stations ... all over northern New Mexico' (Ruppelt 2011: 198), with sighting devices that automatically recorded the time, elevation and direction of any UFOs observed. These stations would be linked, so that any two concurrent sightings would give the UFOs' speed and altitude. Further, this 'visual spotting net' would be linked into the existing radar defence net in the Albuquerque-Los Alamos area, which would be equipped with long focal-length cameras to record any objects located by the radar. And third, there would be instruments in the area capable of measuring 'nuclear radiation, any disturbance in the earth's magnetic field, and the passage of a body ... giving off heat' (Ruppelt 2011: 198). These three sources – instruments for detecting radiation, radar tracking, and the visual spotting stations – would send their information to a central 'UFO command post'. This plan and the budget were approved at ATIC and sent up the system in December 1952 (Ruppelt 2011: 199), although never subsequently enacted.

The 'interplanetary hypothesis' therefore appeared to be being carried by a fair wind. However, it fell at the hands of the scientific panel, which was convened in January 1953.

The aftermath of the Washington Incident (b) the Robertson panel report

Ruppelt gives a circumspect and largely optimistic account of the panel, focussing on the contribution of Project Blue Book and the presentation of its materials, and the scientists' response to these and other evidence (the study of behaviour indicating intelligent control and two pieces of film). The scientists' report, however, rejected the films and the case for signs of intentional behaviour, and found loopholes in each of the fifty best case studies presented: 'all we had was circumstantial evidence … no hardware, no photos showing any detail … no measured speeds, altitudes, or sizes – nothing in the way of good, hard, cold, scientific facts' (Ruppelt 2011: 224). The report added that, if UFOs were a new or undiscovered natural phenomenon, 'the reports of their general appearance ought to follow a definite pattern – [and] the UFO reports didn't' (Ruppelt 2011: 225).

Despite these conclusions, the recommendations appeared more favourable, arguing for continued research into the problem, seeking evidence that would be better than circumstantial, together with mobilizing all kinds of needed scientific expert knowledge, developing an observer network of the type that had been planned, engaging the help of military and civilian scientists, and keeping the American public informed of the research, in order both to dispel the mystery around flying saucers and to hold the Air Force to account (Ruppelt 2011: 225).

Swords (2000: 108ff.) gives an account with both more detail and a different emphasis. In this account, the panel of scientists was not convened by the Air Force but by the CIA, following the order by President Truman at the National Security Council meeting in late July that they investigate the problem of UFOs, with the communications fiasco uppermost. Sparks (2001: 47ff.) puts a version of the same case, playing up the CIA's distrust of the Air Force and inter-organizational antagonisms.[27]

Following Swords' account, the investigation was undertaken by the CIA's Physics and Electronics Division. The initial survey, which included evidence from the Weapons and Equipment Division and from the Psychological Strategy Board (both departments of the CIA), led to

---

27 In Swords and Powell (2012: 170–203), Swords gives a detailed appraisal of the CIA's motives for their involvement with UFOs. In brief, an attempt by the CIA to gain a bigger interest in weapons development and commissioning had been fought off by the Armed Services, and a focus through UFOs on the vulnerability of communications and the potential for psychological warfare allowed the organization to reassert their relevance in technical areas of concern. For background, see Hogan (1998), Montague (1992) and Haines (1997).

a memorandum of September 1952 (headed 'Flying Saucers', reproduced in Swords and Powell 2012: 177–181) which focussed on two problems resulting from the flying saucer situation. The first identified the possibility that the sightings might be controlled by the Soviets for purposes of psychological warfare and that, by making the ideas of flying saucers widely accepted by the American public, they gained a potential for 'touching off ... mass hysteria and panic' (cited by Swords 2000: 109). The second problem concerned the vulnerability of the Air Warning System – both radar screening and visual observation – to the misidentification of potentially hostile incoming flights. A focus on UFOs therefore presented both technical and mass psychological issues which needed to be resolved.

Project Blue Book's optimism, with its belief that the military apparatus might make common cause with scientists and government agencies to 'solve' the UFO problem, was then misplaced.

The CIA investigators made progress on several fronts. They first satisfied themselves that 'the phenomenon was neither American nor Soviet' in origin (Swords 2000: 111); there was no suggestion either of the Soviets' possessing the necessary sophisticated technology or of their active use of superior knowledge of the phenomenon (whatever its source). They also discarded the hypothesis of 'natural phenomena or known types of aerial vehicles' (Swords 2000: 111). They then decided to assemble a group of scientists who could advise how to undertake research and development on the subject, and the Air Force promised to cooperate with this.

Thus far, the account differs little in substance from Ruppelt's telling. At this point, however, the records let us down for, according to Swords, the group that was convened and reported had a different agenda – one of closing down the UFO problem, this time definitively – and we have no documentary evidence of where the decision was made. The panel was chaired by a former CIA employee, Howard Robertson, a nuclear physicist and flying saucer sceptic (Swords 2000: 112), and was composed by members whose 'concern was national security and the cold war' (Swords 2000: 113). And the panel's vital conclusion, from this perspective, was that 'the evidence presented on Unidentified Flying Objects shows no indication that these phenomena constitute a direct physical threat to national security' (Swords 2000: 113). The problems were identified instead as the potential misidentification of real threats, the overloading of communications channels in a crisis, and the enhanced possibility of mass hysteria (Swords 2000: 114).

For good measure, the panel added that, while there were unexplained cases and evidence which did not rule out the possibility of visits to earth by intelligent creatures from other celestial bodies, 'there is nothing in all the so-called "flying saucer" reports that we have read that would indicate that this is taking place' (cited in Ruppelt 2011: 223).

We have then travelled full circle: once again, the interplanetary hypothesis was shelved, and the security issues were foregrounded. The task was no longer to understand the problem as constituted, but to discourage reports and to dampen public interest. The Robertson panel made several recommendations to the security services to counter the risks created by flying saucers, first, that the military should be better trained so as to be able to discriminate between significant reports of potential enemy action and insignificant reports of UFOs and, second, that moves be taken 'to strip the Unidentified Flying Objects of the special status they have been given and the aura of mystery they have unfortunately acquired' (cited in Swords 2000: 115).

With regard to the second recommendation, specific attention was to be given to a programme of reducing public interest in UFOs, using 'television, motion pictures, and popular articles', focussing on cases which promised mystery, but which had been resolved. Experts in mass psychology were to advise on the best means of achieving the desired end, and the advertising and film industries employed in delivering the message. Various networks for dissemination were considered, including schools and clubs. Contrariwise, organizations spreading any views that ran counter to the desired outcome, such as civilian saucer clubs, should be watched because of their potential influence on the public and investigated by the security services for subversive activity.

Swords lastly outlines some of the effects of the Robertson panel report. Once the priority of security issues was established over any investigation of the interplanetary hypothesis, certain moves followed. The earlier proposals of both the Air Force and the panel of scientists for a major extension of practical research were scrapped, as were the possibility of systematic scientific analysis of reports on the one hand and the idea of keeping the public informed of such research on the other. The duty of investigating sightings was shifted to the station-based intelligence officers of Air Defense Command and Project Blue Book was sidelined, with its personnel replaced and once more reduced in number. UFO 'sympathizers' in the Air Force became marginalized, and little energy was expended on investigations. All these moves paralleled the earlier shift from Project Sign to Project Grudge. In short, public relations came to predominate over scientific enquiry as the presiding concern, backed by the scientific community's *a priori* dismissal of the possibility of UFOs, which took over from the engineers' interest in providing solutions to technical problems.

Correlated with these developments, public trust in the military fell; fewer reports were made, going instead to civilian research groups such as the Aerial Phenomena Research Organization (APRO, led by the Lorenzens and founded in 1952), the Civilian Saucer Investigation (CSI) of Los Angeles (founded in 1951), the Civilian Saucer Intelligence of New York (CSI New York), and the National Investigations Committee on Aerial Phenomena (NICAP), the last two founded in the aftermath of the Robertson panel report in 1954 and 1956 respectively.

There was pressure exerted on these civilian groups by security organizations; CSI Los Angeles, 'composed mainly of employees of aerospace industries' (Swords 2000: 119) disbanded in October 1953 after investigation by the FBI. There was particularly pronounced conflict between the intelligence community and NICAP. And Swords cites one officer's statement made to a hearing of the House of Representatives Armed Forces sub-committee in 1960, which 'characterized civilian UFO organizations as being driven by "either financial gain, religious reasons, pure emotional outlet, ignorance, or possibly to use the organization as a cold war tool"' (Swords 2000: 120).

In short, the default position of both the Air Force and the security forces was that UFOs represented no security threat but that they needed to be played down because of their potential psychological effects. More positive – or different – attitudes emerged for short periods, from 1947 to 1948 and from 1951 to 1952, for the most part from engineers, but in these skirmishes between positivists of different stripes, the sophisticated security-minded pragmatists won out over the more disinterested technicians. Questions of mentality rated a higher priority than investigating possible material realities: mind trumped matter each time. The Robertson panel report is the point of decision. Although scientists were given the power to decide, they were not prepared in any way to commit to the interplanetary hypothesis (although, as always, they opted for more research). Yet, within six years (by 1959), they would have constructed something comparable to the hypothesis in NASA and SETI.

VII. Some general conclusions

What can be drawn from this account? We can make four general remarks.

1. Hierarchies and atmospheres

First, we are dealing with a relatively self-contained – though complex – social environment, a hierarchical military organization employing advanced technology, composed exclusively of men with extensive combat experience. In one regard, it was structured by formal bureaucratic procedures, by proformas, by reports of incidents and investigations, filed and stored, by memos, requests and written recommendations sent up the system, and by decisions sent down the system, conveyed by the publication of orders, formation of projects, changes of project status and so forth. These procedures at every level could be used to assist or obstruct initiatives. In another perspective, however, it was constructed by informal 'atmospheres', by collective office behaviour, by monitoring whether a project was favoured or disfavoured by those higher up, and by anticipating changes in fashion from the top down. Questions of atmosphere determined the degree of cooperation experienced in an enquiry and, in the case of Ruppelt's Washington experience (or at least the account he chose to give of the day's events), the lower ranks who defeated his efforts lagged behind the high-ups' renewed concern with the topic.

These two tendencies may have sat uncomfortably together. Ruppelt states that the records do not show where a decision came from in the case of the non-pursuit of one proposed initiative, signalling at a wider level the end of Project Sign: 'I don't know where the plan was killed, or who killed it, but it was killed' (Ruppelt 2011: 57). Changes in atmosphere led more formal decisions and were not recorded. The same is true of the records of the Robertson panel. It is worth remarking that, in this regard, this social world is far more secretive in its working and less well documented than the science fiction milieu, both at the time and in retrospect. And at times, the two tendencies may have come directly into conflict: Ruppelt records two occasions when documents were destroyed by decisions of intelligence officers: copies of the Estimate were incinerated after it was rejected by the Air Force Chief of Staff (Ruppelt 2011: 45), and a recording of the meeting at the Pentagon which resulted in a reversal of policy concerning Project Grudge was later destroyed (Ruppelt 2011: 93). There is a third example of the destruction of a document in the book's opening pages (Ruppelt 2011: 5), which we will discuss in concluding, and a fourth if we include Swords' account of the fate of the Counter-Estimate. The repeated destruction of internal records is a curious activity for an intelligence organization, worth remarking, and may relate to the fact that a hierarchical organization is juggling several functions and has more than one desired objective, the priorities between them shifting in an unpredictable fashion. It also illustrates the claim that, in a world controlled by signs, the past may be manipulated by the destruction of documents. There is no evidence, however, referring back to Melley (2012), of the creation of forged documents in the military.

This hierarchical world was then not simply top-down in its authority relations; as in any hierarchical system, separation of rank was mitigated by interdependence between levels and by circumstantial reversals of power and initiative. A senior officer could only fulfil his duties if those beneath him carried out their work well, not only obeying orders but also making sense of the wider implications or implicit intention behind the orders. The other way about, a good senior officer both took advice from those lower-down and covered for inefficiencies in his men's execution of the orders given on his authority; we can see both processes in General Samford's actions, who had approved Ruppelt's plans for reactivating Project

Grudge (Ruppelt 2011: 115ff.), understanding their rationale, and who, in the press conference following the Washington incident, both backed that rationale and covered for the intelligence failures of his operatives. The earlier meeting, called in response to the sighting of a UFO on new radar equipment at Fort Monmouth, New Jersey, by Samford's predecessor, General Cabell, represents another case in point. Cabell appealed directly for information to Cummings, by-passing intermediate ranks, and Cummings detailed ATIC's minimal response to UFO reports (something he was trying to correct against the current), leading to an abrupt reversal of priorities (Ruppelt 2011: 93). Despite appearances, then, the Air Force was not a closed system; rather, each rank and situation had its own forms of wider accountability, and accountability was never stable nor fully predictable. Higher ranked officers, especially in Washington, were accountable to the press and, potentially, to the attention of politicians, responding to public interest; lower down, and away from the capital, more parochial interests predominated, but always subject to disturbances which had their focus elsewhere.

It is in these interstices, with their uncertainties and small adjustments, that we can locate the improvisations and unpredictability of the system, in short, the genuine creativity of the paradoxically highly ordered system. In this instance, the introduction of a new form of recording – radar traces, in the Fort Monmouth case – provided new possibilities within the experimental system being created within ATIC.

This complex hierarchy, with its combination of formal procedures and informal ways of doing things in response to accountability at various levels, supports the narrative arc of Ruppelt's account, with its periodic alternation of interest in and indifference, or even hostility, to flying saucer reports. An initial engagement focussing largely on potential security issues – the prime concern of the armed forces in peacetime – was eroded by the lack of any forthcoming supporting evidence and the consequent loss of prestige to its advocates. A new surge of interest followed the introduction of a new technology, home-based radar, leading in due course to a repetition of the first disappointment, with no fully substantiated sightings or materials to study. Further technological fixes were proposed, but none gained sufficient backing. Once the CIA's enquiry had become convinced that no security threat could be shown, and that supporting evidence was in short supply, the Air Force was constrained to seek to rid itself of the embarrassment of press interest and the public suspicion that it knew far more of the matter than it was letting on. These oscillations – between engagement and disinterest, a focus on research and a concern with pragmatic effects – constitute the crucible of production of the image, the practical mechanism of its evolution.

2. Engineers, scientists, and the public

Second, if the production of an object of thought within military-technical circles consists in these repeated shifts from causes to effects as the principal focus (and briefly back again, under the impetus of technological innovation), we might ask why the Air Force people were in the main content to leave undecided the question of whether flying saucers existed or not; provided they represented no security threat, secondary questions of prestige and convenience determined policy. They shared this attitude, of course, with the wider population; only scholars, in particular, natural scientists, feel the need to settle the question definitively one way or the other, normally employing the Morton's fork of 'fiction or error?' with respect to forms such as flying saucers. The problem becomes temporarily acute, however, when new technologies such as radar provide positive evidence; questions of 'truth' then reappear with force.

Part of the answer lies in the fact that the military are technicians and engineers, with every aspect of their profession shaped by advanced technologies. In this regard, it is important that Ruppelt was concerned exclusively with what he regarded as 'reliable' witnesses, which meant technicians, military and civilian. This motif of reliable testimony recurs throughout the book and is widely shared in the period, and its other face is the effective exclusion of testimony from ordinary citizens. A *de facto* division emerged early on between reliable sightings, attributed to technicians, where the crucial question concerned testing various potential 'natural' explanations such as weather balloons, misidentified aircraft, atmospheric inversions, birds in flight or reflected sunlight, which had to be eliminated, and less reliable sightings coming from the public, where the first questions concerned the personality of the informant and the quality of the data provided – 'determinable psychological quirks' and 'insufficient data' (Ruppelt 2011: 10). This division was formalized in the reorganization of Project Grudge, which involved the coordinated creation of a proforma for investigations and of a data base on IBM punch cards with the details collected, including the personality of the observer, together allowing a 'mode of operation' through a profile of similar cases (Ruppelt 2011: 118–119). In this fashion, however, a great body of information was excluded, the sightings of ordinary citizens.

It was excluded because it could not serve the rational technical ends being employed. Ruppelt tried his best to incorporate it; he advocated a more open approach to the press to gain more input from the public, to allow the possibility of combining multiple sightings and of gaining data through triangulations (Ruppelt 2011: 117), although he later admitted this had not worked. He also employed a newspaper clipping agency (Ruppelt 2011: 137). But ordinary reports did not lend themselves to statistical techniques.

We can say that the engineers were good at improving techniques and creating more data, but that they did not ask where their object came from, nor where they had derived the categories which defined their object in its broad outlines; rather, each successive technique introduced produced its effects. Pulp science fiction shaped early Air Force responses – as in the Maury Island incident – and each new technology and technique introduced (after the initial fall-away in interest) gave further substance to these responses. Radar produced tracking to match sightings and mapping produced sequences of tracks or sightings; each new artefact was a potential condensation of what we might call a hybrid object. The application of statistics did not alter the status of the object. No matter how much technology was applied, we have a positive object in a wrapping that was full of surprises but with acknowledged features, waiting to be discovered.

3. The life of hybrid objects

Third, what are the wider ramifications of these hybrid objects being given substance by the efforts of technicians? The technology supplied authority to the reports of unidentified objects, which played in a context created by the demands of the press and politicians. Ruppelt gives good material on the internal divisions within the Pentagon staff, who had, by the time of the mid-June 1952 briefing, fully taken on the hybrid objects, without perhaps, because of their situation, fully appreciating the potential for development that accompanied them. The division revolved around whether to go on gathering information before coming to any conclusions or whether to be more proactive. In the latter case, the proposal was to accept the existence of UFOs, to form a more interventionist team, drawing scientists into the project, and to control public perceptions by reducing or cutting off information to the press. Swords (2000) refines this account and accentuates the rivalries.

As we know, the two sides compromised on that occasion, ordering the design of new equipment to collect better data. But the crucial feature of this plan was, as it turned out, to have accepted that their task involved the shaping and control of public opinion through action on the media. Swords' account brings out the slightly later plans – practical or otherwise – for security interests controlling and shaping the civilian population's focussing on, grasping and understanding certain contemporary events; these centred on the use of advertising and cinema, the placing of press articles, consideration of means of altering children's ideas, and intimidating where possible organizations whose aims went counter to these aims. These aims and activities were in the context of the Cold War and deep distrust of the loyalty of liberal milieus (expressed in the contemporary witch hunt against Communists), and a widespread belief in the significance of mass psychology and the potential for a good society to become rotten from within. We might note that the world view given expression by pulp magazines was widely shared. In short, these new objects played out in tensions between the Pentagon, the Press and politicians, with control of the popular mind as the stake; in this setting, questions of mass psychology trumped any research or intelligence interests.

These activities are best seen as an extension of the production of effects of UFOs by technical means: the becoming-real of the fictional object through the introduction of new technologies. Just as the technologies produce new information, an aspect of that production is the control of the dissemination of information, so that a yearning for contact and communication with alien life forms (even in the form of self-defence) is combined with a fear of that communication going astray. The hope of communication is largely lived out through preventing its going to the wrong recipients, so that, in an age of information, the task of security involves home propaganda. Neither side in the Pentagon debates would have disagreed with this point of view. The only issue was how to do it effectively.

4. The characteristics of UFOs

Fourth, and concluding the lessons which may be drawn from Ruppelt, we may ask what does this phenomenon, which is being given substance by this series of technological innovations and wider social effects, look like?

In the first place, it appears in a series of 'firsts': the first sighting, the first radar tracking, the first tracking of a climb, the first matching of a visual sighting with radar tracking, the first series of sightings of either kind over a timed and mapped trajectory, the first tracking recorded on more than one radarscope, and so forth. These 'firsts' create the sense of a progressive revelation as we get nearer to the possibility of understanding the nature of the phenomenon.

Then, any incident has a similarly constructed form, including such elements as a period of preparation as the location is identified, with multiple sightings in the area and the growing interest and anticipation of various interested groups, followed by the assembling of the players at the site with, in the Washington incident, intelligence off-balance and the multiple radar bases, followed by the event and associated sightings, on and off-screen. The narrative form pulls together evidence of which any piece, taken in isolation, is rather weak, but which is bolstered by reliable witnesses – radar operators, intelligence officers and fighter pilots.

Next, there is a playing out of human forms construed as possible evidence of alien intelligence within the frame of the technological narrative. The progressive revelation of 'firsts' hints at some alien intelligence trying to contact human minds in a progressive fashion. And, at the same time as these technical effects emerge, there appears to be a matching set of reactions on the part of the flying saucers: in the first place, the UFOs appear to know a good deal about human activities, appearing over military sites or over-flying political buildings, or returning on the same day of the week or at the same time. And in the second place, it is as if the flying saucers are playing with human perceptions, calling attention to themselves, allowing themselves to be pursued, but never caught, revealing more of themselves in a progressive manner. It is possible to interpret the developments as evidence of other minds, and as displaying considerable interest in and knowledge of human intentions, even perhaps anticipating human actions, including the possibilities of knowing when a radar fix on them has been made and of mind-reading the pilot's intentions in a confrontation. Technical properties imply mental correlates.

The playful 'supernormal' element was evident in the Washington incident, where the reported behaviour of the UFOs was at first laconic, when they allowed themselves to be monitored, before they sped away, drawing attention to themselves by flying over the White House, a security target above all others, and finally disappeared, never being intercepted or examined from close to. It was as if they were teasing, or at least had some communicative intent. Likewise, the behaviour of the UFOs in the second Washington incident is worth remarking: the pattern, of gathering lights that dispersed at human approach only to gather elsewhere, shifting repeatedly and vanishing with the dawn, reminds the hearer of folktales of goblin festivals. Later writers (Keel 2014; Vallee 2014; Strieber 1987, for example) explore along this track.

In short, there was no conspiracy of positive knowledge, even though Air Force intelligence subscribed to a policy of secrecy and the manipulation of information (or public education) at home. They were thoroughly enmeshed in a world where new technologies shape human ends and could not escape their part in the drama of the becoming-real of ideas, as new objects and the means of their apprehension emerged simultaneously. Ruppelt concludes his chapter on the Washington incident with a defiant flourish, offering us the best 'good' sighting in his collection, on the very day of the press conference which signalled the longer-term mothballing of his project. But the real story lay elsewhere, in the productions of evolving collective representations and the life forms produced at their margins.

A ghost story

Ruppelt offers confirmation of these conclusions by prefacing his entire account with a detailed anecdote which has the structure of a ghost story, an ambiguous narrative in which the mix of hierarchy, discipline, authority and prejudices that characterizes a military organization play their parts. It is as if he wishes quietly to tell the reader of the social world in which he worked, although ostensibly the topic of the book concerns evidence and proof.

The story came from Ruppelt's meeting with an intelligence officer at an American fighter base. The commanding officer of the fighter group 'believed that UFOs were real' because, as a former pilot, he had faith in his pilots who had chased UFOs, and he had seen the signals on the radar (Ruppelt 2011: 1). This colonel exemplified the combination of newly deployed technology and faith in testimony from trustworthy and experienced sources which Ruppelt saw as being crucial to the revival of military interest in UFOs in 1950–1951 (see Ruppelt 2011: 6). The UFO-sceptical intelligence officer passed Ruppelt a report concerning a particular sighting. It contained several elements: an object first appeared on the radar, flying initially at 700 m.p.h., but then slowing to 100 m.p.h. There were insufficiencies in the equipment – it did not measure altitude – and the target faded on the radar; it was assumed to be climbing. Two planes were sent up and directed from the ground, but by the time they reached the (disputed) height, the target had been lost on the radar. The two planes were told to search at lower heights, and the lower found an object flying close to the speed of sound which the pilot tracked and got good sight of. He had however lost radio contact at this point both with his fellow pilot and with ground control. The object, which was round and flat, started to pull away from the pursuing plane and the pilot, being outpaced, opened fire. On this, the object 'pulled into a climb and in a few seconds was gone' (Ruppelt 2011: 4). The pilot also climbed, contacted his partner on the radio, and the two planes returned to base.

On his return, the pilot was interviewed, first by his squadron commander and then by a group consisting of the squadron commander, the colonel and the intelligence officer. The squadron commander accused the pilot of shooting off his guns and fabricating a story to cover up. Testimony was called from other officers as to the man's mental condition and customary behaviour (there had been previous 'minor incidents') and his fellow pilot was interviewed. The latter said he had received no radio calls from the low flying aircraft, and the first pilot said he may have been using the wrong channel.

The intelligence officer wrote up the report of the interviews, but was then told by the squadron commander, after consultation with his executive officer (the colonel), to destroy the report and not to send it further up the line to ATIC, which would have been standard procedure. The intelligence officer nevertheless showed the report to Ruppelt before destroying it.

Ruppelt comments that this story is typical of UFO reports: some facts can be gleaned from it, but 'no matter how thoroughly you investigate the incident', the substance of the story – a 'something' seen and shot at – 'can never be positively identified' (Ruppelt 2011: 5).

The story confirms the enduring characteristics of these reports. The whole story is only possible because of technology, in this instance, the deployment of radar for domestic air defence, and the preparedness of the military – taking the form of F86 fighters – for the defence of national air space.

Then, the debriefing reveals the hierarchical structure of authority in the Air Force, which may be expressed both as a clash of personalities between the pilot and his squadron commander and by the quasi-legal business of testimonies, questioning, character references and expert opinions. In the end, the colonel must decide, out of sight of any witnesses we have access to, how to treat the report and whether to register it or suppress it. We cannot know what motives were at work. They may have been pastoral, letting the pilot off the hook and placating the squadron commander, or political, suppressing a credible sighting which might have caused panic if widely reported; they might have been in accordance with wishes from higher up, though at variance with standing orders or, on the contrary, in defiance of higher policy.

And last, the account has the structure of a ghost story: while there are indications of data that might be shared – radar signals and radio communications – any sense of shared experience is lost in the presence of the disputed object. It fades and disappears from the radar and, when the planes separate, radio communication breaks down. The machinery fails in its presence. Moreover, the object displays uncanny properties, both physical properties, of speed and acceleration and the ability to vary its flight path, and mental properties, showing even powers of anticipation, correlating its behaviour with that of the pursuer and taking evasive action at the precise moment of being fired upon. It not only shows properties of mind, of intention and foresight, but also appears to interact with the mind of the temporarily isolated pursuer, just as it can affect equipment.

Ruppelt then not only gives a history of the early period when flying saucers first appear and are, so to speak, given substance; he also prefaces this history with a 'warning to the curious' in which the commanding officer (in this regard recalling the Master of a College in an M. R. James' tale) orders the destruction of any evidence and record of the appearance. We only get to hear the tale through a series of over-hearings – a story told to Ruppelt by a man who was present when the witnesses were questioned … Under certain circumstances, intelligence work is subverted into quite another genre.

VIII. What have we learnt?

What have we learnt? The narrative has a clear structure. An argument about the possibly interplanetary origins of flying saucers first emerged in Air Force circles by the end of 1947, arising from a series of negatives – the belief that no known design could achieve the performances claimed, and that the human form could not stand the resultant stresses. Those involved filled out the negatives by recourse to the stereotype of an advanced civilization, with the same trajectory as human civilization in terms of technical and moral development, but far in advance of our own.

The filling-out drew on two mechanisms. In the first place, the invention of a name that gave unity to a range of reported sightings, first 'flying saucers', created by a journalist in the Arnold case and gaining worldwide use, then 'flying disks' and a range of variable terms within official documents – unidentified 'aircraft' or 'object' or 'flying object' – hardening into 'Unidentified Flying Objects', coined by Ruppelt and adopted by the Air Force, scientists and technicians and then being used by the public. A later technical term invented by Alan Hyneck was 'Close Encounters' of various kinds (see Hynek 1972). This 'nominalism' was backed up, in the second place, by adoption of the method of residues, which presumes that when all misidentifications, hoaxes and pathologically inspired reports have been eliminated, what remains are examples of the class identified by the name.

This named residue was given substance and coherence by a series of technical fixes, centring around the expansion of a home radar defence system but with additional elaborations, and by the business of building an operational profile through the development of questionnaires and the technical means of handling them statistically. The residue in this fashion could take on a life of its own, allowing in the case of each incident the joining of the dots made up of anticipations, sightings of various kinds and coincidences of unrelated features to produce a series of always unresolved puzzles, and permitting, in the case of attempts by the press and saucer organizations and the like, the suspicion that there was a conspiracy to conceal a pattern to these events, a suspicion which was also open to being elaborated into a well-defined and recognizable narrative.

There is then a process at work which is prior to representation and gives the 'material' which representations can shape. In this instance, irrespective of whether individual investigations might have developed another, more appropriate mode of approach and analysis, interpretative possibilities were generated which could simultaneously be claimed to be both 'real' and 'fictitious'. These interpretative possibilities have their own history; they took on new characteristics according to circumstances, and the options were favoured or contested following shifts in local political context. There had been a short period during which the 'interplanetary hypothesis' had gained a foothold in some military and scientific circles. By 1953, concerned scientists and security operatives had however reached a consensus that the contested phenomena would neither yield definitive evidence nor produce any practical outcome – they represented no threat. But by that time, the 'imaginary object prior to representation', if we may call it so, with its equally possible representations as reality or fiction, had a sufficiently autonomous existence to prolong its independent life outside the structures that had given rise to it; it had its own credentials and could follow its own trajectory.

To map out the story in terms of concepts borrowed from Rheinberger (following up the remarks at the end of Section V), an image seeded in the early post-War years was made the subject of a first hypothesis, the interplanetary hypothesis, in Project Sign. This epistemic thing took form in the period of Project Grudge, the first reversal, when emphasis shifted from research to questions of mass psychology and reputation, and then rebounded with the deployment of a new technology, radar. The experimental system hinted at in 1948 was developed in the first years of Project Blue Book, 1951–1953, with the construction of spaces of representation, in which the image was given a range of characteristics. By the time of a second reversal of fortune, around much the same issues, the image had taken on sufficient form to become a technical object, a more or less inert constellation of elements which could be taken up in different experimental cultures, by writers, ufologists, and space scientists, and evaluated according to the pattern of true or false and, if false, fiction or error.

In short, in a high-tech, military world, the split between engineers and security men, one focussed on machines, the other on minds, generated all kinds of signs. In such a world, technical effects such as unexplained radar traces can produce exaggerated responses, and similar responses can reappear with each new technical development.

Discussion

Flying saucers were produced in a precise milieu and period within the Air Force. This work was not undertaken intentionally: there was no programme to design and launch flying saucers, although they represented an amalgam of contemporary experimental technical ideas. They emerged instead in an apparatus of reports, memos and investigations, which led to organizational changes and the attribution of budgets, and to the assembling of records and the development of equipment to record and measure the phenomena, and then resulted in a series of conflicts in interpretation, hypotheses put forward, policy decisions and reversals of decisions, conflicts between factions, the inflection of certain careers, the destruction of documents, and a series of attempts by committees to shape accounts of past history and to redirect public opinion, if necessary by deception and propaganda.

If you wanted evidence for 'flying saucers' or 'disks' – which is the form life from elsewhere took on in the late 40s and early 50s – you should look less, perhaps, to the always-ambiguous material of reports of sightings and more to this remarkable series of organizational effects, leading to disturbances of a local but sometimes quite acute kind, which are well-evidenced and available in the now fairly open archives of the organizations in question. If we look for evidence not in objects and isolated acts but in networks and patterns of events, there is a good deal to be considered.

Probably the best way to understand flying saucers is as a scientific hypothesis which was tested in various ways but ultimately discarded as lacking convincing supporting evidence. While early Air Force interest was triggered by visual sightings, reported for the most part by pilots, the issue was given definitive form by the deployment of a home radar system across the United States around 1950. This was an enormous technical operation, involving the development and rolling out both of radar systems and of communications networks throughout the home territory to defend against a potential Soviet nuclear attack. It was the next big defence-funded programme after the Manhattan Project, with all its implications for the leap forward of associated technological innovations, a central part of economic development as well as defence. It led, because of the need for fast communication – 'early warning' – to the computer industry in the 1960s. This deployment of radar on home soil, as a side-product, appeared to produce objective evidence of what came to be known as 'Unidentified Flying Objects' (UFOs), so that, as well as seeing lights in the sky, there would be report, in the same area and at roughly the same time, of signals on radar screens, potential aircraft. The Air Force applied standard intelligence procedures to these UFOs, as a small-scale operation within the department which had the business of tracking and investigating the properties of enemy aircraft and missiles.

Hence the range of practices already listed, from memos to major rows, which gave form and substance to the mysterious objects being sought; though no saucer was ever grounded or captured, nor any individual machine identified, nor even clearly photographed, the existence of these objects can be traced through their effects in a whole range of human activities both regular and anomalous, involving not only the military and security organizations, but also the press, politicians up to the level of the President, and many members of the public. There is a considerable literature to be investigated.

My point here is a simple one: if you go back to the early period – 1947–1953 – and look at the documents, flying saucers or UFOs are a product of the constellation of various military, industrial, technological and scientific interests of the time, and life elsewhere takes this form and no other because of its site of production. Above all, these forms are not some kind of myth invented in the margins of society which sensible and responsible people must shake off; they are indeed the expression of a contentious but orthodox hypothesis – termed the 'Interplanetary hypothesis' at the time – that these machines come from other planets, other planetary civilizations, and are intelligently guided.

The emergence of the interplanetary hypothesis can be traced through the documents. Once the sighting of what came to be known as Unidentified Flying Objects became accepted as a security problem to be resolved, a sequence of questions followed. Initially, is this a secret weapon being developed by another branch of the Armed Forces about which we have not been informed? Once that had been denied, a second question followed: is it a Russian weapon we do not know about being tested or deployed? But no reason could be given for testing new weapons over American territory, although speculation about 'psychological warfare' played a considerable part in the debates, and, again, no convincing evidence emerged. So, the third question followed, is it 'interplanetary'? A standard set of intelligence techniques worked out in the Second World War were set to work and applied to the problem thus identified, and men transferred from working on Russian weapons in Korea, machines which combined a high level of performance with new technology, thought to show the American aircraft in a different light and comparable in this regard to UFOs.

We need to know in more detail, then, where the 'interplanetary hypothesis' came from, and the precise form by which ideas of intelligent life were projected onto and into space and life forms imagined which show a reciprocal interest in human civilization: the hypothesis comes from Theosophy, which gave a narrative shape to the extraordinary advances by the physical sciences and evolutionary biology in the last part of the nineteenth century, and whose cosmology was disseminated through pulp science fiction in the first part of the twentieth.[28]

In this essay, we have followed the hatching of the interplanetary hypothesis and its moment of glory in security circles, using Ruppelt's history to reconstruct the stages of its formation and condensation. There is, however, more to the story; this episode is only one part of a chain. While the interplanetary hypothesis was not supported, and the history of its elimination from the military agenda is a delicate tale, by the time it was discarded it had taken on a life of its own. The other essays in the series are concerned with tracing that independent life.

28 This is the business of the second essay.

Bibliography

Arnold, Kenneth and Ray Palmer, *The Coming of the Saucers: A Documentary Report on Sky Objects That Have Mystified the World*, Boise, WI, Published by the Authors, 1952.
Barrow, Logie, *Independent Spirits: Spiritualism and English Plebeians, 1850–1910*, London, Routledge & Kegan Paul, 1986.
Benjamin, Walter, 'The Work of Art in the Age of Mechanical Reproduction' [1936], in Walter Benjamin, *Illuminations*, edited by Hannah Arendt, London, Bodley Head, 2015.
Bioy Casares, Adolfo, *The Invention of Morel*, New York, New York Review of Books, 2003 [1940; E.T. 1964].
Borges, Jorge Luis, 'Tlön, Uqbar, Orbis Tertius', in *Labyrinths*, Harmondsworth, Penguin, 1970.
Braude, Ann, *Radical Spirits: Spiritualism and Women's Rights in Nineteenth-Century America*, Bloomington, Indiana University Press, 2001 [1989].
Buchan, John, *The Three Hostages*, Harmondsworth, Penguin Books, 1966 [1924].
Clark, Jerome, 'Foreword', in Colin Bennett, *Flying Saucers over the White House: The Inside Story of Captain Edward J. Ruppelt and His official US Airforce Investigation of UFOs*, New York, Cosimo, 2010 [Originally published as *American Demonology. Flying Saucers over the White House etc.*, Manchester, Headpress, 2005].
Clark, Jerome, *The UFO Book: Encyclopedia of the Extraterrestrial*, Detroit, Visible Ink Press, 1998.
Considine, Bob, 'Air Force Insists Imagination, Reflections Have Tricked Public', *International News Service Column*, New York, 16 November 1950.
Considine, Bob, 'The Disgraceful Flying Saucer Hoax', *Cosmopolitan*, 33, January 1951: 100–102.
Crane, Tim, *The Objects of Thought*, Oxford, Oxford University Press, 2013.
Festinger, Leon, Henry W. Riecken and Stanley Schlachter, *When Prophecy Fails*, London, Pinter & Martin 2008 [1956].
Franklin, H. Bruce, *War Stars: The Superweapon and the American Imagination*, Amherst, University of Massachusetts Press, 2008.
Ginna, Robert (with H. B. Darrach Jr), 'Have We Visitors from Space?' *LIFE Magazine*, 7 April 1952.

Hacking, Ian, *Representing and Intervening: Introductory Topics in the Philosophy of Natural Science*, Cambridge, Cambridge University Press, 1983.

Haines, Gerald, 'CIA's Role in the Study of UFOs, 1947–1990', *Studies in Intelligence* 1 (1), 1997: 67–83.

Hall, Michael David and Wendy Ann Connors, *Captain Edward J. Ruppelt: Summer of the Saucers – 1952*, Albuquerque, NM, Rose Press, 2000.

Heard, Gerald, *The Riddle of the Flying Saucers: Is Another World Watching?* London, Carroll and Nicholson, 1950.

Hinsley, F. H. et al., *British Intelligence in the Second World War. Its Influence on Strategy and Operations*, London, H. M. Stationery Office, 1979–1990.

Hogan, Michael, *A Cross of Iron: Harry S. Truman and the Origins of the National Security State, 1945–1954*, New York, Cambridge University Press, 1998.

Hynek, J. Allen, *The UFO Experience: A Scientific Enquiry*, New York, Ballantine Books, 1972.

Jacobs, David Michael, *The UFO Controversy in America*, Bloomington, Indiana University Press, 1975.

Jenkins, Timothy, *Of Flying Saucers and Social Scientists: A Re-reading of When Prophecy Fails and of Cognitive Dissonance*, New York, Palgrave Macmillan, 2013.

Johnson, DeWayne B., 'Flying Saucers – Fact or Fiction?', Master's Thesis, University of California at Los Angeles, 1950.

Jones, R. V., *The Wizard War, British Scientific Intelligence 1939–1945*, New York, Coward, McCann & Geoghegan, 1978 [Published in Britain as *Most Secret War*, 1978].

Keel, John, *Searching for the String: Selected Writings of John A. Keel*, Andy Colvin (ed.), Seattle, Metadisc Productions & Point Pleasant, WV, New Saucerian Books, 2014.

Keyhoe, Donald, 'Flying Saucers Are Real', *True*, 11–13, January 1950a: 83–87.

Keyhoe, Donald, *The Flying Saucers Are Real*, New York, Fawcett Publications, 1950b.

Keyhoe, Donald, *Flying Saucers from Outer Space*, New York, Henry Holt, 1953.

Kittler, Friedrich, *Gramophone, Film, Typewriter*, Stanford, Stanford University Press, 1999 [1986].

Kittler, Friedrich, 'Media and Drugs in Pynchon's Second World War' (1987), in Kittler 2013: 84–98.

Kittler, Friedrich, *The Truth of the Technological World*, Stanford, Stanford University Press, 2013.

McLaughlin, Robert, 'How Scientists Tracked a Flying Saucer', *True*, 25–27, March 1950: 96–99.

Méheust, Bertrand, *Science-fiction et soucoupes volantes: une réalité mythico-physique*, Rennes, Terre de Brume, 2007 [1978].

Melley, Timothy, *The Covert Sphere: Secrecy, Fiction, and the National Security State*, Ithaca, Cornell University Press, 2012.
Montague, Ludwell Lee, *General Walter Bedell Smith as Director of Central Intelligence*, University Park, PA, Pennsylvania University Press, 1992.
Packard, Vance, *The Hidden Persuaders*, Harmondsworth, Penguin Books, 1964 [1957].
Peebles, Curtis, *Watch the Skies! A Chronicle of the Flying Saucer Myth*, Washington, Smithsonian Institution Press, 1994.
Pynchon, Thomas, *Gravity's Rainbow*, London, Vintage Books, 2013 [1973].
Rheinberger, Hans-Jörg, *Towards a History of Epistemic Things: Synthesizing Proteins in the Test Tube*, Stanford, CA, Stanford University Press, 1997.
Riesman, David, *The Lonely Crowd, a Study of the Changing American Character*, New Haven, Yale University Press, 2001 [1950].
Ruppelt, Edward J., *The Report on Unidentified Flying Objects: The Original 1956 Edition*, New York, Cosimo Classics, 2011 [Originally Doubleday & Co., 1956].
Samuel, Wolfgang, *American Raiders: The Race to Capture the Luftwaffe's Secrets*, Jackson, MI, University Press of Jackson, 2004.
Shalett, Sidney, 'What You Can Believe about Flying Saucers', *Saturday Evening Post* 30 April 1949 & 7 May 1949.
Skully, Frank, *Behind the Flying Saucers*, New York, Henry Holt, 1950.
Sparks, Brad, 'Ruppelt's Coverup', in Thomas Tulien (ed.), *Proceedings of the Sign Historical Group, UFO History Workshop*, Scotland, The Sign Historical Group, 2001: 40–49.
Strieber, Whitley, *Communion: A True Story: Encounters with the Unknown*, London, Arrow Books, 1987.
Swords, Michael, 'Astronomers, the Extraterrestrial Hypothesis, and the United States Air Force at the Beginning of the Modern UFO Phenomenon', *Journal of UFO Studies* 4, 1992: 79–130.
Swords, Michael, 'Donald Keyhoe and the Pentagon', *Journal of UFO Studies* 6, 1996: 195–211.
Swords, Michael, 'UFOs, the Military, and the Early Cold War Era', in David M. Jacobs (ed.), *UFOs and Abductions*, Lawrence, KS, University Press of Kansas, 2000: 82–121.
Swords, Michael and Robert Powell (eds), *UFOs and Government: A Historical Inquiry*, San Antonio, Anomalist Books, 2012.
Toffler, Alvin, *Future Shock*, New York, Random House, 1970.
Toronto, Richard, *War Over Lemuria: Richard Shaver, Ray Palmer and the Strangest Chapter of 1940s Science Fiction*, Jefferson, NC, McFarland & Co., 2013.

Vallee, Jacques, *Passport to Magonia: From Folklore to Flying Saucers*, Brisbane, Daily Grail Publishing, 2014 [1969].

Virilio, Paul, *War and Cinema*, New York, Verso, 1989.

Winkler, David, *Searching the Skies: The Legacy of the United States Cold War Defense Radar Program*, Langley AFB, VA, United States Air Force Air Combat Command, 1997.

Index

advanced military technologies
    atomic energy 79, 114, 115
    early warning system 79, 114, 116, 151
    missiles 41, 44, 79, 116, 122
Air Defense Command (ADC) 114, 115, 119, 137
Air Material Command (AMC) 80, 85, 110
Air Technical Intelligence Center (ATIC) 73, 80, 104, 112, 119, 133, 140, 147
aliens 50, 60, 62
American Air Force 65–153
American Air Force: communications fiasco 121, 131, 134, 136
anti-Communism 82
Arnold, Kenneth, 91, 95, 100
atmosphere, changes in 74, 110, 138–139

Bioy Casares, Adolfo 52–64
broadcast of *The War of the Worlds* (Orson Welles) 130

chronological approach 21, 70, 77
CIA (Central Intelligence Agency) 75, 80, 88, 132–135
civilian UFO organizations: Aerial Phenomena Research Organization (APRO), Civilian Saucer Investigation, Los Angeles (CSI Los Angeles), Civilian Saucer Intelligence of New York (CSI New York), National Investigations Committee on Aerial Phenomena (NICAP) 137
Clark, Jerome 7, 75, 77, 131
communication 7, 15, 22, 24, 36, 37–42, 51, 56, 144, 148, 151 *see also* information
computers 38–40, 51, 116, 120, 151
copies and originals 58–59
covert sphere 68, 83–84, 106
Crane, Timothy 13–14

engineers (cf. security) 111, 124, 137, 141–142, 150
epistemic thing 68–69, 72, 104, 124, 150 *see also* image
errors and fictions 1, 8–10, 11–13, 13–14
Estimate (Air Force) 85–90, 104–105, 108, 110, 139
event, theory of 18–19, 28
experimental cultures 69, 150
experimental systems 68–69, 72, 122–123, 140, 150
eyewitnesses, expert and civilian 82

factions: pro- and anti-saucer 76, 107, 112
FBI (Federal Bureau of Investigation) 102, 108, 137
Festinger, Leon 18–20
Film Noir 47
flaps 124–127
flying saucer clubs 20, 111, 138
foo-fighters 81
Franklin, Bruce 78, 80

ghosts, ghost stories 146–148
ghost rockets 81, 108
Ground Observer Corps (GOC) 115, 116, 119

image 1, 23, 24, 30, 63, 66, 70, 97, 104, 123, 124, 141, 150 *see also* epistemic thing
imaginary (cf. real) 1, 8, 16, 27, 32, 42, 51, 64, 68, 84, 149 *see also* virtual
incidents
    Chiles and Whitted 88, 91
    Coyne 5–7, 18, 21, 30
    Fort Monmouth 112, 117, 140
    Gorman 92
    Mantell 87, 91
    Maury Island 91–103
    Washington 124–138
information 20, 27, 29, 38–51, 64, 66, 67, 69, 123 *see also* communication
intelligence work (cf. scientific research) 2, 23, 70–73
interplanetary hypothesis 23, 76, 78, 87, 91, 124, 131–133, 136, 138, 149, 150, 152–153
inter-service rivalries 75, 110, 118

Jacobs, David Michael 75, 95, 106, 109
Jones, R. V. 40, 71–72, 118

Keyhoe, Donald 77, 109, 124, 130
Kittler, Friedrich 38–51, 84
Korean War 2, 23, 72, 73, 105, 109, 115

Manhattan Project 80, 118, 151
mass psychology 76, 105, 106, 120, 136, 143, 150
media, new 22, 36, 39
Melley, Timothy 66, 82, 83–84, 106, 130
'men in black' 101

National Security Council 134
natural object and social convention 10, 11–13
nominalism 149
non-anticipatory approach 21

operational profile 149

Palmer, Ray 95–97, 99, 101–102
paranoia as a social condition 38, 42, 46–50, 51
Peebles, Curtis 75, 95, 96
Pentagon 80, 83–90, 110–112, 124, 126, 128–129, 132, 143
President of the United States 131, 134, 152
press, local and national 82, 97
press articles
    Considine 106, 111
    Ginna 124
    Keyhoe 109, 124
    McLaughlin 109, 124
    Shalett 106, 124
Project Blue Book 70, 73, 76, 124–126, 132–137, 150
Project Grudge 73, 90, 91, 104–106, 109, 110, 112, 117, 119, 137, 139, 142, 150
Project Sign 73, 85, 87–90, 91, 109, 111, 119, 137, 139, 150
psychological warfare 82, 108, 109, 134, 135, 152

radar sightings 73, 108, 117, 120, 122, 125, 130, 131
radar sightings, combined radar/visual 113, 119, 131
radar
    Distant Early Warning System 116
    Home Defense System 73, 117
    Lashup System 115
RAND 80, 88, 90, 114

Index

real (cf. imaginary; virtual) 1, 5, 8, 10, 11, 13, 14, 16, 19, 27, 30, 32, 46, 51, 56, 59, 60, 64, 67, 68, 86, 120, 143, 145, 149
representation, problems of 10, 16, 17, 42, 48, 69, 123, 149–150
Residues, method of 105, 120, 122, 149
Rheinberger, Hans-Jörg 67–70, 123, 124, 150
Robertson panel report 75, 76, 124, 133–138, 139
Ruppelt, Edward 65–153

science fiction 7, 8, 10, 20, 21, 24, 28, 29, 32, 37, 42, 49, 98, 103, 139, 142, 153
scientific research (cf. intelligence work) 2, 23, 70–73
second order categories 43, 45, 50
Second World War 21, 22, 38, 39, 40, 72, 118, 152
security (cf. engineers) 71, 111, 124, 137, 141–142, 150

Shaver mystery 95, 97, 102
shift in object and framework 17–18, 30, 67
sightings and testimonies 21, 25
space of representation 69, 122–123, 150
Sparks, Brad 75, 105, 128, 134
spiritualism 100
spy balloons 121
Strategic Air Command (SAC) 116, 121
Swords, Michael 67, 75, 77–81, 85–90, 96, 107–113, 117, 120, 121, 131–138, 143

technical object 70, 100, 124, 150
technological fix 117–122, 140
technological innovation and relation to media 35–51
Theosophy 24, 26, 37, 111, 153
time travelling 42, 43–46, 50

virtual 27 *see also* imaginary

Winkler, David 113–117

Mini Series: Images of Elsewhere
TIMOTHY JENKINS

Vol. I
Flying Saucers: An Introduction

Vol. II
Religion and Science Fiction

Vol. III
Martian Linguistics

Vol. IV
UFO Reports

Vol. V
Alien Sightings

Vol. VI
Images of Elsewhere

www.ingramcontent.com/pod-product-compliance
Ingram Content Group UK Ltd.
Pitfield, Milton Keynes, MK11 3LW, UK
UKHW021323180426
11947UKWH00017B/1403